BEASTLY BEAUTIFUL

by Dara England

Also by Dara England

THE ACCOMPLISHED MYSTERIES

Accomplished in Murder

Accomplished in Detection

Accomplished in Blood

THE AMERICAN HEIRESS MYSTERIES

Death on Dartmoor

Murder in Mayfair

CONTEMPORARY FICTION

Love by the Book

The Magic Touch

Chapter 1

"I MIGHT HAVE WORK FOR YOU tonight."

The remark was offered by a dark stranger with a clean, sophisticated look about him. Everything from the full-length charcoal coat and gloves he wore, to the light briefcase he carried spoke of money. His black hair was longish but slicked back in a tidy style. The toes of his shoes sticking out from beneath his black slacks were shiny enough to reflect the glow of the single streetlight overhead.

Teagan drew her eyes from those fancy shoes and returned them to the stranger, who still loomed over her expectantly.

"What kind of work?" she asked warily.

"The sort that pays well for someone who knows how to keep her mouth shut."

He leaned forward, and for the first time, the light from the overhead lamp fell across his face. Teagan couldn't help staring. He was younger than she'd first thought, probably in his thirties, but still had a good ten years ahead of her. His face was darkly attractive with strikingly chiseled features that went well with his broad shoulders. A pair of thick, black brows arched over deeply set eyes that were all but lost in shadow. Teagan thought she caught a glimpse of a steely glint within those shadows, and then he tilted his head and his features were lost to her again.

"I haven't all night to await your answer. Are you interested in earning a little money or not?" His voice was deep and easy, belying the emotions Teagan sensed lurking beneath the surface. Although his posture and words were smooth, she somehow felt there was a nervous energy beneath his controlled movements, some unnamed feeling rattling and trying to escape the emotional prison he had constructed for it.

Teagan didn't want it to get out now. She shivered under the bite of winter wind. Uneasily, she cast a glance up and down the empty alleyway, looking for a casual passerby. Even a cop showing up to tell her to move along would be welcome just now.

At her nervous gesture, the stranger laughed—a low, chilling sound Teagan thought held a ring of malice. Unexpectedly, he dropped into a crouch beside the bundle of rags and newspapers making up her bed. Taken aback by the sudden motion, she would have scrambled to her feet immediately had not some inner sense warned against it. When stalked by a dangerous animal, the worst thing to do was break into a run.

The stranger must have read something of her thoughts. When he spoke his voice had lost any trace of humor. "I can assure you that you won't be asked to do anything dangerous or difficult. The task I have in mind for you is something of a simple yet very secret nature."

"I don't keep secrets so good," Teagan said stiffly.

The stranger seemed amused. "Forgive me. I didn't think in your position you'd be choosy about how you landed a roof over your head and a bite of food in your stomach." His mocking gaze took in the cardboard box that provided her temporary shelter, along with the bulge of crumpled, discarded newspapers she'd shoved inside her sweater for insulation against the bitter cold.

Teagan was in no condition to take offense at his boldness. Besides, his reference to food and shelter had caught her attention. Her belly ached from having had nothing all day but a half eaten cheeseburger from a garbage can.

"What kind of chore did you have in mind?" she asked, meeting the stranger's gleaming gaze with an effort. There was something about those black eyes that made her own want to slide away from them. What was she getting herself into?

At her question, he smiled craftily, as if he already knew he had her. "The kind of task that pays five hundred dollars."

"Five hundred—" Despite herself, Teagan's eyes bugged out.

"Caught your interest, have I?" he observed coldly. "Good. No doubt you're wondering why I offer so much."

Teagan held her tongue. She was wondering

exactly that.

He continued. "You might say the extra amount is for the tricky part of the job—the silence. If you and I were to enter into a little...business arrangement, it would hinge on the stipulation there are to be no questions asked. Not now. Not ever. And you could speak of our deal to no one else. Is that clear?"

It wasn't. "Do you want me to help you rob a bank or something?" she asked. "How much trouble am I risking for this money?"

He raised dark brows. "That remains to be seen," he said, straightening. "But if you can't handle not knowing, this won't be the job for you. Again—"

"I know," she finished. "The no questions asked clause."

"You catch on quickly," he said. "Good. Do we have ourselves an understanding?"

No. She still had no idea what she was agreeing to. She didn't speak her reservations aloud however. The promise of those five hundred dollars drew her in like the scent of food to a starving man. She had the uncomfortable and vaguely alarming sense the stranger knew it too.

She took a final moment to contemplate his expensive clothes, his cultured accent, and the faint scent of high-priced cologne drifting from him. He looked like a wealthy and influential citizen, for all his aura of darkness. Surely whatever he had in mind couldn't be anything too terrible. He was giving her time to think, she realized, but she had no doubt he was already confident of her response. He had chosen his victim—or maybe his accomplice—well.

"I—I'll do it," she said, forcing herself to voice the decision before she had any more time to think. "I'll accept the—the work, and I'll keep all the conditions." Why did she have the ominous feeling she was agreeing to her doom?

He didn't allow her time for second thoughts. "Very good." His tone was so even it was difficult to tell whether he was pleased or surprised by her decision.

His fingers were tapping rapidly on the handle of his briefcase. They had been doing so since he'd first approached her and began this odd conversation. Now he cast a brief glance overhead, to where the last of the evening twilight was quickly fading from the sky. Down in the alley, beneath the shadow of the city's towering skyscrapers, dusk had already fallen. Again, Teagan sensed a pent-up energy inside him. What, she wondered, could be making a man like this nervous—if indeed fear was the powerful emotion she sensed surging within him.

"We've little time to waste," he announced, snapping his attention back to her. His attitude was so cool she could almost believe she was mistaken in thinking him preoccupied with internal concerns. "Come," he said, rising to his feet. He offered a gloved hand, but seemed unsurprised when Teagan pretended not to see it, scrambling upright unaided. "Follow me," he ordered simply and turned away, leading her toward the mouth of the alley.

Teagan's palms were sweaty and her heart thundered as she followed slowly after him, feeling as if she were walking toward some unreal fate. She'd just sold herself. She knew that. But for what purpose?

Chapter 2

OUT ON THE STREET, THE dark stranger hailed a cab. Teagan thought this seemed an odd way for such a well-dressed man to travel. Somehow she'd had an image of him climbing into the back of a sleek black car and gesturing a chauffeur to carry them to their destination. They were silent for the duration of the short ride. Teagan wasn't sure if the stranger was mindful of the extra pair of ears in the front seat, or if he simply had nothing more to say to her.

She cleared her throat abruptly. "What, uh, what can I call you?"

His tone was bored. "My name isn't important. If you have to call me something, sir should do well enough."

Sir? Teagan had never encountered such arrogance. She hadn't called her own father sir. Nevertheless, for five hundred dollars, she supposed he was calling the shots...

He didn't seem interested in learning her name. In

fact, he displayed no curiosity toward her whatsoever as he leaned toward the front seat. "Turn in here," he instructed the cab driver.

Teagan peered out the window to see they were turning into the parking lot of one of the most luxurious apartment houses in town. In fact apartments hardly seemed the right word to describe these towering residences. They were for the fabulously wealthy. The city's elite. She glanced in awe at her companion before turning her attention to the imposing structures ahead. Who was he anyway, this Sir? A politician? A wealthy businessman?

She had little time to take in the full effect of the landscaping and architecture. She only had a brief impression of its grandness, and then they were pulling to a stop before the doors of the nearest building. Sir stepped out of the car, Teagan scrambling after him. When he opened his wallet to pay the cab driver, she caught a glimpse of the thick wad of cash inside. The bill he handed the man was a fifty, yet he didn't even wait for change. Suddenly she knew what a paltry sum the five hundred dollars she'd been promised was to him. She should have held out for more.

The lobby of the building they entered was brightly lit from within. A doorman in a blue jacket held the brass double doors for them as they stepped inside. Teagan couldn't remember anyone ever holding a door for her in her life. She knew if she'd tried to enter this elegant place in any company but that of the wealthy man called Sir, those fancy doors would have been slammed in her face and locked.

Indoors, she looked with wonder at the marble tiled floor and the luxurious furnishings arranged around the lobby. Sir stalked past it all with the disinterest of someone who was so accustomed to opulence he had long since learned to take it for granted.

Teagan was trailing behind and scuttled to catch up to his long strides. They stepped into an elevator that was like a fancy little room of its own, with a small chandelier hanging from the ceiling and a potted plant standing in one corner. The walls of the elevator were glass, offering a view of the levels below as they were swiftly carried to the top floor.

She felt briefly dizzy, looking down from such a height while moving, and closed her eyes, waiting for the nausea to pass.

When the elevator arrived she expected to find herself looking out into some sort of corridor. Instead, the doors opened straight onto what looked like a living room.

She couldn't hide her astonishment. "So, like, just anybody could jump into the elevator and take a ride up to your living room?" she asked.

"It doesn't work quite that way," he said, but failed to explain further. "You can get out now," he added, as she stood in the doorway, staring.

Teagan had been frozen in place long enough that the elevator doors were about to close again. She advanced just far enough forward to enter the room, but didn't move in any further as, with a soft *ding*, the elevator doors closed behind her. Awe at her surroundings left her immobilized. She had never seen a penthouse before, let alone been invited into one. The entire living area seemed almost as large as the downstairs lobby and could have easily held a hundred people. What parties he could hold up here, Teagan thought.

Fancy white leather sofas formed a square in the sunken center of the living room, and other luxuriant furnishings were tastefully scattered around the room. Teagan found herself marveling at imaginary price tags on everything she looked at and made herself stop. Decorative art was displayed in niches along the walls, much of it under glass. She couldn't imagine owning anything valuable enough to keep under glass in your own home, and so supposed these pieces must be priceless.

Maybe art was a passion of Sir's. Or, possibly, he was just fond of using it to show off his wealth. Either way, there were several low tables arranged throughout the room, holding wooden carvings or small statues. A life-sized sculpture in black marble of a pair of lovers entwined in one another's arms stood just to Teagan's left.

"You admire the piece?" Sir broke into her thoughts. "It was a gift from the very talented artist, the late Jean Phatteu."

"You knew Jean Phatteu? The Jean Phatteu?" Teagan asked.

He smiled at her open surprise. "I wouldn't call him a personal friend," he answered. "But I made his acquaintance once or twice in Paris."

Teagan stared at the sculpture with a renewed

respect, until she became suddenly aware of Sir's laughing eyes on her. Simultaneously, she remembered it wasn't just a piece of art before her. It was also a naked statue. Flushing, she averted her gaze to the next marvel, an immense chunk of black rock, rising up out of the floor near the center of the room and reaching almost to the ceiling. It took her a moment to realize it was a fountain with a sheet of water cascading across its smooth surface.

Scarcely aware of what she was doing, she moved further into the room. There was a fully stocked bar along one wall and at the opposite side of the room a kitchenette, divided from the rest of the space by a waist high brick wall. Kitchenette was as ridiculous a name to apply to the vast area as living room had been for the other.

If she had been alone, Teagan would have taken the time to explore the space more fully, and maybe even poked her head into a few of the doors letting out of the main area. As it was, she abruptly remembered she was gaping, open-mouthed, as if she were inspecting the palace of a magnificent pharaoh.

Her mouth clicked shut, and she shook away her amazement. It was just a house, that was all. A fancy place to lay your head at night.

Sir was watching her with an expression in his mocking eyes that made her wish she had treated her surroundings more casually. Clearly, he thought her some sort of hobo stumbled in from the slums, and wholly flabbergasted by her good fortune at landing in such a place.

"Well, I'm here," she said, chagrin making her sound prickly. "When do I start earning my five hundred bucks?"

"Very soon," he said smoothly.

Removing his dark coat, he cast it over an opulently decorated creation Teagan could only dub loosely as a coatrack She seemed to find herself coming up short of names for lots of things since stepping off the elevator. Sir was yet another sight that was putting her at a loss for words. Beneath the full-length coat that had concealed him, he was dressed in a blue silk shirt and dark tie over black slacks. He somehow looked just as formidable in his casual attire as he had when buttoned up under a long coat. The sleeves of his shirt were rolled up to the elbows, displaying an impressive looking pair of forearms. Teagan caught herself wondering if the rest of the package were as pretty as the pieces she'd seen and then looked away, mortified he might have guessed at her thoughts by the expressions playing across her face.

But he had already turned his back on her. "Follow me," he said, disappearing through one of the doorways adjoining the living area.

Follow him to what, exactly? Despite the hesitant thought, Teagan obeyed. As abruptly as that, her decision was made. There was no turning back.

Chapter 3

THE NEW ROOM TEAGAN ENTERED was a sort of smaller living area. The spacious area had what was probably meant to seem a more intimate atmosphere, with an open fireplace along one wall, and a couch and pair of armchairs drawn up before it. A few shelves lined the walls, again displaying more art treasures, along with stacks of books. Nevertheless, the feel of the place was far from casual. At least, it wasn't the sort of room where Teagan would feel comfortable plopping down and putting up her feet.

An entire wall was devoted to a floor-to-ceiling sized entertainment center, displaying an immense television screen and a sound system with more knobs and buttons than Teagan could imagine uses for. Catching her gaze lingering over the entertainment center, he seemed annoyed at the distraction, quickly flicking a switch on the wall near the door. The entertainment section of the room sprang into action, doors sliding closed and walls folding in on themselves until, a few seconds later, all that remained was a smooth, seamless looking wall of dark wood. Teagan felt as if she stood in the presence of magic.

A simple clap of Sir's hands dimmed the lights to a softer glow. Teagan noticed there were no light fixtures hanging from the ceiling. Rather, the edges of both floor and ceiling were lit by the glow of canned lighting set into the walls. The softer, yellow illumination provided an informal effect, but Teagan was far from relaxed by it.

Sir led the way to the fireplace, where he waved Teagan to a seat on the sofa. The cushions were so thick she immediately felt swallowed by the furniture as she sank into its embrace. Sir didn't sit, but planted himself before the fireplace. He must have turned a knob somewhere near the mantelpiece because a row of thick orange and blue flames suddenly sprang up from the bottom of the fireplace.

Teagan wondered if it was pathetic that she could be so easily awed by the mere presence of fire and moveable bits of furniture. Then again, maybe it wasn't solely the special effects that had her under their spell. As Sir regarded her from his stance before the fireplace, she found herself shrinking a little under his dark gaze.

Nearby, the sharp ticking of a pendulum clock over the mantel broke the silence. Sir's eyes moved to the clock, and his fingers began tapping impatiently along the top of the mantelpiece, in time with the ticking noise. It was his only indication of irritability, yet Teagan felt something in him had changed from the time they entered this room.

She was abruptly reminded of the uneasy, impatient sense she'd felt emanating from him in the alley. Something dark flickered in his eyes, but she felt whatever passions stirred below his surface had not been awakened by her presence. Something about that clock disturbed him, she thought, as she witnessed his eyes being drawn to it seemingly against his will.

The sudden chime of the hour startled Teagan, and she jumped in her seat. The hands on the clock had moved to seven. Sir wasn't affected by the noise, as she had been. He appeared prepared for it. Braced, even.

Teagan felt a cold, ticklish sensation, akin to fear, start to creep its way up her spine. What was going on here? She suddenly had the odd sense there was something unimaginably awful hanging over both their heads. She had the abrupt urge to leave this fancy penthouse and its strange, intense inhabitant far behind her.

With an effort, she controlled the desire to leap to her feet. *You're imagining things*, she told herself. This whole unreal place and situation had stirred her naturally overactive imagination to full flame, that was all. To quash her fear, as she waited for Sir to come out of his eerily silent mood, she concentrated on the reward to come and on planning what would be the first thing she ate when she got out of here with her fists full of cash.

"It's time." The low words, uttered in a tone of surrender, of inevitability, caught her attention. She had no idea what time Sir was referring to, but by now she had an idea it wasn't anything he welcomed. "I will explain your task now," he said.

"Okay." Teagan shifted nervously under his gaze.

"It's very important you pay attention to all of my instructions and follow them to the letter. The slightest deviation could mean—" He stumbled and seemed to catch himself abruptly. "It could affect your pay," he finished. "You won't receive a cent if the job isn't done to my specifications. Do you see the small, silver box resting on that desk?" he asked.

Teagan's gaze followed his to a heavy oak desk resting in a shadowed corner of the room. Because of the magnificence of the rest of the space, she hadn't, until this moment, given that area more than a passing glance. Now she rose and followed at a distance, as Sir led her to the desk.

"Lift the box," he ordered when Teagan stood before the desk.

She did as she was told. The little box of decorated silver was about the size and shape of a musical jewelry box, and felt cool and heavy in her hand. As she lifted it from its resting place, she saw a small brass key lying hidden beneath.

"You are not, under any circumstances, to open this box," he instructed coldly, as if noticing her curiosity. "I simply want you to note the placing of the hidden key for future reference."

"I have noted it," Teagan said matter-of-factly, matching his seriousness. What was all this leading up to?

"Then come with me." He led her out of the room and back into the larger open living area.

He next directed her attention to a smaller, but still very expensive looking, sound system in this room. Removing a CD from a nearby rack he popped it out of its protective case and inserted it into the CD player. "I already have this set up as I want it," he said, pushing several buttons on the player. "The track is selected, and I've programmed it to repeat. All you'll need to do is push the play button at the right time."

This was terribly strange. He was paying her all that money to come up here and push a button on his CD player—something he could do very easily? But aloud all she said was, "And at what time would that be?"

"We'll get to that in a minute," he said. "I'm not finished yet. Notice that door." He pointed toward a door at the far corner of the room.

It stood out because it was constructed in a different fashion than the other doors letting off from the living area. It was iron banded, like a dungeon door out of a medieval castle, and painted red.

"That's my study," he said. "I keep all of my most important papers in there, and it's vital you never enter. You mustn't so much as peek inside or you will lose your reward. I don't take kindly to prying." His tone was cutting as he said this, making Teagan instantly nod agreement.

"One last thing," he continued, moving on to the kitchen. He opened the doors of a stainless steel fridge set into the wall. The interior shelves held enough food to feed a lone man for a month. "This—" He indicated the bottom shelf. "—is where I keep the wine. Remember it."

"Um, okay," she said, thinking this was getting weirder and weirder.

He opened the doors to his kitchen cabinets. "Here is where you'll find a full table setting, including a wine goblet. There is silverware in the drawer and a cloth for the table. You can set up a place on the table in the corner there."

"I'm getting a little confused," she said.

"Don't be. Now comes the part where I give you your instructions."

He left the kitchen and she trailed after him. Despite his words, he didn't appear in any hurry to get to the point. Pausing before a long row of red curtains running the full length of one living room wall, he tugged on a cord Teagan hadn't previously noticed hanging among the draperies. Instantly the curtains drew back, displaying a window that made up an entire wall of the room.

The window looked out over the smaller buildings below, offering a breathtaking view of the city at dusk. Cars streamed by on the crowded streets. Pedestrians jostling one another on the sidewalks looked like tiny dots from here. Neon signs flashed in the distance, the sky on the horizon joining their array of color with its own fiery hue as the last sliver of sun sank down out of the sky.

Teagan stood close to the window, gaping at the scene below. "It's fantastic," she murmured aloud, caught up in wonder.

"Is it?" He leaned one forearm against the glass

and gazed out over the rooftops. "I used to think so." From out of nowhere, a glass of brown liquid appeared in his hand. He seemed unaware of it, studying the darkening horizon. There seemed an air of resignation about him, and yet Teagan also felt a deeper underlying excitement. Whatever it was he thought of, it was something he both dreaded and anticipated. "I have to go out," he announced abruptly. "You'll complete your tasks without me." He downed the drink in his hand in a single gulp and slammed the glass down on the edge of a low table nearby.

"But—but you haven't told me anything yet," Teagan protested as he whirled and moved away, suddenly appearing to be in a rush. She scurried after him. "I don't even know what my task is."

He was already snatching his coat off the rack. "It's pretty simple, just listen closely and do exactly as I say," he said, agitatedly. "Go into the den and sit down to watch the clock. At about…" He hesitated, casting a measuring eye toward the darkening sky outside the long window. "At exactly seven-thirty," he corrected himself, "you'll get up and retrieve the brass key I showed you from beneath its hiding place under the silver box. I'll remind you again—don't think for a moment about opening the box. I will know if you do."

His words held such a threatening note that Teagan immediately dropped any notions she might have harbored of taking a secret peek inside once he was gone.

He continued, his words picking up speed as he threw on his coat, as if he already couldn't wait to be on his way. "You will bring that brass key into this room and use it to lock the door to my study from the outside. Don't interrupt me," he added when she opened her mouth to protest.

"No questions asked," he reminded her shortly. "You'll lock my study and replace the key exactly as you found it. You will then start the CD player on the track I have it set on. Leave the volume as it is. Don't readjust anything. Next, you will remove the dishes I showed you from the kitchen cabinet and lay out a single place setting at the table. Pour a goblet of wine and leave that on the table as well. No food. Just the wine. You will then leave my apartment, having touched nothing else. Go back to your cardboard box in the alley and speak of this night to no one."

"And then I'll be finished?" Teagan asked. This was the weirdest assignment she'd ever heard of in her life. She couldn't imagine why on earth any of these strange things he had ordered should be worth five hundred dollars to anybody.

"No, that's not all. At precisely six o'clock in the morning, you must return to this apartment to undo all of your work. You won't see me then, but I will know if you fail to complete the tasks. Turn off the music, unlock the study door, replace the key, and then put away the table setting. After that, your work will be over. We will not meet again."

"But what about the part where I get my five hundred dollars?" she asked, as he moved to the elevator and punched the down button. "If you're not here when I leave tonight and you're still gone in the morning, how are you going to pay me?"

The doors opened and he stepped onto the elevator. "You'll know when the time comes," he said. And then he was gone, the doors shutting in front of him. The last glimpse Teagan caught of his face revealed a pained, distorted expression, as if he'd already dismissed her and turned his thoughts to whatever unpleasant occasion lay ahead of him.

Chapter 4

L EFT TO HERSELF, TEAGAN RETURNED to the room he had referred to as the den and sat, much as he had instructed her to, before the pendulum clock atop the mantel, waiting for it to chime the half hour. This was the oddest night she'd ever experienced.

When the appointed time arrived, she moved to the desk and slipped the brass key out from beneath the silver box. She hesitated over the box for the space of a breath, trying to muster the nerve to disobey his command and lift the lid. He had said he would know, but how could he? Surely it was a bluff.

All the same, she let the box be and moved into the living room. Again, she was assailed by temptation as she slipped the key into the lock of the study door. She felt a strong desire to crack the door a little and see what was so special it needed these strange precautions. Surely he would never know if she took the briefest of glances into the room.

Pausing, she rested an ear against the thick wood.

No sound stirred from within. But then, why should it, she asked herself. It was a study. The room probably just contained a lot of shelves of books and a desk full of papers. She thought fleetingly that if there was anything of value inside she might be able to make away with it in Sir's absence. Yet she seemed to hear his voice again, ringing in her ears. *I will know.* The coldness of his tone made it hard to doubt his sincerity, even as impossible as his claim seemed. Again, she resisted temptation and left the door closed.

She next followed his instructions on starting the stereo. At once, the heavy strains of a piece of classical music blared from the twin speakers. The music was so deafening she was tempted to turn the volume down several notches but on second thought, recalling his order against readjusting anything, didn't. Let his neighbors complain and get him evicted. It wouldn't be her problem.

She moved on to the kitchen. Here she found herself confronted once more by the full refrigerator and no one in sight to see what she did. Under the weakness of her aching belly, she told herself surely he would never notice the difference if one or two small things went missing from there. He had more food than he could eat before it spoiled anyway. She slipped a couple pieces of fruit and a slice of bread out of the back of the refrigerator and tucked them inside her sweater. Then she returned to her tasks.

This was probably the weirdest—even eeriest— part of the evening. She felt very uneasy, filling a crystal goblet with the rich colored wine and arranging the glass alongside pieces of fine china across the low kitchen table. With the frantic notes of an angry sounding musical piece crashing in the background, Teagan felt like she was performing some sort of strange ritual as she laid out the single place setting on the empty table. She wondered whom it was for. Sir? Some mystery guest who had yet to arrive?

She tried to shake both the questions and the anxious feeling from her mind as she wound up the last part of her task. Replacing the brass key where she'd found it, Teagan hesitated one last time in the center of the room. Looking around her, she felt as if the stage had been set tonight for some frightening invisible drama that had yet to play out. All of her tasks—each of the simple acts she had carried out exactly as he ordered—appeared innocent enough on their own and yet together, she couldn't shake the feeling they spelled something very wrong. She wondered fleetingly if Sir might not be a little unbalanced in the head. The notion made her eager to leave.

Her hands were trembling as she pressed the down button on the elevator. As she stepped between the doors, she almost wished she'd never agreed to this whole bizarre bargain. Maybe she wouldn't come back in the morning to finish up after all. Maybe she would let him keep his money.

Back in her cardboard box in the shadowy alley, she devoured her bread and fruit with a speed born of long hunger. She shivered in the cold wind. It was at times like this she almost regretted her decision to avoid the homeless shelters. Unfortunately those were just the sorts of places her family might look for her. And being found wasn't on her agenda. Not even if hiding on the streets meant starving.

All she needed was the chance to find her feet, she promised herself for the thousandth time. A job was sure to turn up soon, and then she'd be able to get her life in shape. And she didn't care what the work was. She'd waitress, she'd wash dishes, anything. But until then...

She curled up in her bed of rags, shuddering beneath the onslaught of the cutting wind, but at least knowing the comfort of a full belly for the first time in days. Trying to work a little warmth into her freezing fingers and toes, she lay awake and remembered the soothing heat of the fireplace in Sir's den and the softness of the thick carpet beneath her feet. Then she thought of the stocked refrigerator and cursed herself for not having taken more food.

She couldn't sleep that night. Cold and fear for the future kept her awake. By the time the blackness of the sky was beginning to give way to a pale gray in the east, she knew her decision was made. She was going back. She had already done most of the work last night. It would be foolish not to return and claim her reward.

It was a short walk to Sir's apartment house. It took her so little time to reach her destination that the moon was still up and a bare scattering of stars twinkled in the lightening sky when she arrived. She had warmed herself a little with the exercise, but unfortunately had worked up a raging hunger as well. Last night's snack was just a torturous memory now. Maybe it would have been better if she hadn't eaten at all.

She didn't give any thought to how she was to get into the building until she found herself standing before the doorman. The neatness of his uniform and the skeptical expression on his face when he saw she intended to enter reminded Teagan that last night she'd had Sir here to gain her admittance. But there was one stroke of luck in her favor. This was the same man who had held the door for them last night.

She gave a sketchy explanation of having done some work for the gentleman in the penthouse the night before, and how he had told her to come back again in the morning. To her relief, he accepted the explanation without question. Was Sir always doing things this eccentric? Then again, maybe the doorman was just used to a parade of female visitors on their way up to the penthouse. She wouldn't be surprised. Sir was good looking, rich...a magnet for certain kinds of women.

She passed quickly through the fancy lobby, feeling uncomfortably out of place as she stepped into the glass elevator. She was getting used to the view down, or at least she was no longer sickened by it, as the elevator shot upward to the top floor.

She found the penthouse just as she'd left it. The unsettling piece of music was still crashing over the sound system. The table setting rested where she had left it, to all appearances, having remained untouched throughout the night. Even the goblet of wine was still full. Maybe Sir's mystery visitor had never arrived. Certainly Sir, himself, didn't seem to have returned yet.

Glancing around at the empty apartment, Teagan felt her nerve rise enough she contemplated raiding the refrigerator again. She could remember a time when she had drawn the line at stealing. That was a long time ago however. Her brief stint on the street was already teaching her she could do a number of things for food she had never thought herself capable of before. Besides, it wasn't as if a man like Sir would miss just one or two items from his overflowing kitchen.

She wrestled with all of these thoughts as she cleared away the spotless dishes, replacing them in the cabinet. Casting a surreptitious glance around her, she threw her head back and emptied the wine glass. No use dumping it down the drain. She hesitated over the dirty glass, and then left it in the sink. She wasn't being paid for housekeeping. Besides, the spotless state of the rooms evidenced a capable housekeeping staff was frequently on hand.

It was a relief to turn off the blaring music. After so much noise, the silence descending suddenly over the room was unnerving. Teagan remembered the eerie feeling of the night before, but did her best to set it from her mind. She wouldn't be frightened away—not before she received her money. As she entered the den, a glance at the pendulum clock told her it was still a few minutes until six—the hour she had been instructed to return and fulfill her tasks. The sky, visible through the long living room window, was still almost black.

Never mind, she told herself. There could be no harm in her having gotten an early start. She removed the key from its hiding place under the silver box and retraced her steps to unlock the red door to the study. She didn't hesitate this time to put her ear against the door. After last night's weird scenario with the table setting and the untouched wine, locking a simple room now seemed the most unremarkable part of her routine.

Returning to the den, she slipped the brass key back into its hiding place. Her task was complete. Now she was left with the question of what to do with herself until Sir returned. She had no intention of leaving without those five hundred dollars firmly in hand. Briefly, she contemplated stocking her pockets again from the refrigerator.

But what if he should somehow find out? Would the fact she had been stealing from him somehow preclude their arrangement? He had said she would receive no payment unless she followed his instructions to the very letter, and swiping food from his kitchen had certainly not been a part of his instructions. Besides, she reminded herself as her stomach grumbled in rebellion, a short while longer and she would have enough cash in her pockets to walk into any restaurant in town and fill her face with all she could eat.

No, more stealing was definitely out. To kill the time, she found herself pacing before the fireplace, listening to the tick-tock of the pendulum clock. She remembered how disturbed Sir had been by that clock last night. The memory of his dark expression unnerved her so much she sought distraction. Her gaze fell on the little silver box.

Almost furtively, she crossed the room until she stood before the desk. Even though she knew there was no one home, she nevertheless found herself casting a wary glance over her shoulder as she reached a curious hand to hover over the lid.

I will know.

She shook her head. He was bluffing. How could he possibly know?

Quickly, before she could lose her nerve, she threw open the lid. It was a musical box. A cheery tune began to play the moment the top was opened. Teagan leaned forward to peer inside. The inside of the box was red-lined...and empty. Teagan frowned. She didn't know what she had expected—jewelry maybe, or a secret stash of cash. But why on earth would he have made such a fuss over the opening of a box, if it stood empty? Unless...

Unless it had been some kind of test to see how well she followed orders. *I will know.* No. He couldn't know. And yet Teagan found herself stepping back nervously, retreating from the little silver box as its tune wound to an end. In the ensuing silence, it struck her. He would know because he had wound the box.

He knew in what place the tune should begin again the next time he opened the lid. It was rather a genius test actually, she admitted to herself. Too bad it wasn't genius enough. She too had an ear for music, and she remembered where the tune had begun. All she had to do was rewind the box until the song started in the exact same place.

Reaching for the box, she heard a soft footfall behind her.

Chapter 5

WHO WAS IT, COME TO catch her red-handed? Sir? Or his mystery guest of last night? Whirling, Teagan slammed into a solid chest. A pair of strong hands gripped her roughly by the forearms, their hold painfully tight. Teagan couldn't have stifled a muffled squeal even if she'd thought to try. Steely dark eyes gazed down on her from a face contorted by rage.

Teagan almost didn't recognize Sir from last night, so changed was his appearance. His hair was wildly mussed and hung down in black strands before his face. His clothing was ripped and blood smeared. There was no knowing whether the crimson stains came from his own flesh or someone else's.

"What are you doing?" he growled, reddened face twisted in anger. An evil, unreasonable fury drove him, Teagan thought frantically. She trembled to find it directed at her. Looking down she saw the large hands clamped around her arms were smudged with blood still oozing from his torn fingertips. The source of his bloodied shirt?

The pulse pounded in her forehead so she thought she might faint. "I—I just wanted to open—I was going to put it back like it was," she stumbled over herself, trying to explain. His blazing eyes registered no understanding of the words.

"It's not dawn!" he shouted in her face. "I told you not until six o'clock!"

Teagan was having difficulty standing, so weak had her legs suddenly became beneath her. "I—I'm sorry," she gasped out, fear paralyzing her mind too fully to let her think of anything else to say. Whoever or whatever had suffered his wrath before, drawing the streaks of blood smearing his clothes and hands, she didn't want to share their fate.

"Sorry?" he grated, his voice sounding for a moment more animal than human. Something bestial flashed within the depths of his black eyes and Teagan had the wild, terrifying notion there was no longer a man lurking behind those eyes, but a rabid animal. Something indefinable in him had changed. Sir was no longer in control of this body.

And in the same instant that realization struck, she had the sudden terrifying notion her life depended on her ability to bring him back to himself at once. In this enraged state, he was not above killing her.

She forced a steadiness into her words that belied the horrified sensations rushing through her body. "Sir, I don't think you know what you're doing right now. Calm down please. It's only a little box, and I didn't mean any harm by opening it. No damage has been done, has it? No one has been hurt."

That last remark may have been a little premature but already she felt her soothing words had penetrated some barrier, for something in the man opposite her altered abruptly. She felt it the moment his grip loosened so his fingers no longer dug like claws into the skin of her upper arms. Slowly, carefully, he removed his hands from her. Suddenly, there was space between them.

His voice was low and thick when he spoke. "You… you should've waited. Until after dawn." Even as he spoke the accusing words, the first orangey glow of morning's light slanting through the living room's long window lit up the doorway behind him.

As if his simple words had been all the explanation required, he stepped away from her. Not until then did Teagan's shaky knees buckle so that she collapsed to the floor. The Sir of last night would probably have helped her up. The Sir of a few moments ago—the beastly personality that wasn't really Sir—she didn't know what he would have done. But the Sir of this morning simply turned his back and walked away.

The set of his shoulders as he disappeared through the doorway was now a posture of exhaustion. Whatever he'd been up to all night, combined with their brief encounter just now, seemed to have sapped the strength from him. Cautiously, Teagan kept an eye on his retreating form as she attempted to pull her shaky legs back beneath her. Her hands were trembling, she noticed. Her whole body was experiencing such a rush of weakness as her adrenaline slowed that she'd be lucky to crawl to the door, let alone walk there.

Although it defied every demand of her shaken mind, she forced herself to stay where she was, drawing slow, deliberate breaths until her trembling lessened. There was no telling what would happen to her if she passed out now on this man's floor. She had an idea she would never be heard from again.

Slowly, as the initial rush of panic wore away, she became aware of the pain of bruises in her arms. he could almost still feel his fingers sinking into her flesh like talons. She suspected the next time she looked in a mirror she would find deep purpling marks there.

She peered through the doorway to see Sir, illuminated by the light of early morning, collapsed in an armchair with his back toward her. He was sitting upright, but his attitude was so quiet she almost thought him asleep. Her mind letting go the last vestiges of her previous frightened state, she began forcing her thoughts and her body under control again.

This could all be explained away in some rational manner, she told herself, even as her heartbeat slowed to a normal rate and the weakness leaked out of her body, to be replaced by a healthier strength. He was drunk, she decided. That was what had happened. A long night of partying had driven away the intelligent, controlled man of last night, replacing him with this wild creature. It was pathetic, really, how a few drinks brought a dignified man down to this level.

Carefully, she rose to her feet, finding her legs much stronger this time, and crept to the doorway. Spying on him now, he seemed harmless enough.

His skin was pale in the morning light; the side of his face visible to her from this angle looked strained and weary. Teagan felt not an ounce of sympathy for him. After his wild behavior, he deserved to suffer the effects of a good hangover. She did, however, find some comfort in his weakened appearance. The Sir she looked on now was not in any condition to give chase should she make a sudden dash to the elevator.

Which was exactly what she did. He made no move to stop her as she skirted quickly around the spot where he sat slumped in his chair. He spoke not a word as she scuttled to the elevator and slammed one nervous hand over the down button. Ordinary drunkenness or not, there was something about this man's presence that would never cease to unnerve her.

The elevator took its time in arriving, and she found herself pounding again at the little glowing button even as she cast anxious glances over her shoulder. If she expected Sir to suddenly lift his head and show an interest in stopping her, she needn't have worried. He seemed neither to know nor to care about her presence. After what seemed an eternity, the elevator doors slid open with a *ding*.

Just as Teagan set her first foot inside the doors, she was startled by a sudden masculine voice. "It's in my coat pocket," Sir unexpectedly stirred himself enough to say. "The money's in my coat pocket." His words didn't sound slurred, just heavy with exhaustion.

Teagan hesitated, half on the elevator and half off. Torn between fear and greed, the two emotions that had been her tormentors since she first laid eyes on this man, she cast a fleeting glance from Sir, reclining in his chair, to the coatrack only a few feet away.

Tossing caution to the wind, she made a break for the coatrack. How could she not, with five hundred dollars at stake? She kept an eye on Sir, who never moved from his spot, all the while she dug through the pockets of the single coat hanging on the rack. It was a shorter gray jacket, not the full-length black one he had left in last night. That coat was nowhere in sight.

A hasty exploration of the outside pockets turned up a thick wad of loose bills. Briefly shocked to find him as good as his word, Teagan quickly pocketed the cash, uncounted. Time enough for that later once she'd put this strange man and his creepy apartment behind her. Stepping onto the elevator, she breathed a sigh of relief when its doors closed and she felt herself being carried downward. She couldn't forget this night fast enough.

Chapter 6

AND FORGETTING WAS EXACTLY WHAT Teagan did over the following weeks. With the money she had earned in that one night, she put herself up in a cheap motel with enough groceries to last a week. In the beginning she meant to be frugal, to live carefully in order to stretch the money out as long as possible. But somehow those five hundred dollars began dwindling away pretty quickly.

She soon found herself back on the streets with only a few dollars left in her pockets. There were more important necessities than shelter, she decided, and invested what money was left in warm winter clothing and a thick wool coat to keep off some of the chill during those long nights spent sleeping under park benches or in abandoned alleyways. Even the food money she had set aside eventually evaporated until, one night, she found herself once again huddled with an empty belly, trying to keep warm under a blanket of newspapers in an alley not far from the one where she had first encountered Sir.

The difference this time was that above all those newspapers and her new thick coat was a fresh sheet of snow sparkling under the moonlight. It might have been pretty to look at, this new, hushed world of freshly fallen snow, but it certainly wasn't pleasant to sleep under. As she lay there shuddering at the biting gusts of wind, Teagan's mind went to the money she had spent and worked over plans for how she could get more of it.

A dark, insistent corner of her mind pointed out that she knew one limitless source of cash. Pushing the thought aside, she burrowed deeper under the snow and tried not to think of it. After the last time, she thought, nothing in the world—not even the possibility of food and shelter—could tempt her to return to that awful place. After her experience in Sir's apartment, she would rather have turned just about anywhere else for help. But her options were few and the longer she contemplated her memories of that night, the less unpleasant they began to seem when compared to the very real possibility of freezing to death in a lonely alley.

It wasn't that night but the next evening Teagan found herself finally standing before the doorman of Sir's fancy apartment, trying to finagle her way in. She'd had enough. Her limbs were in a constant state of stiffness from the unceasing cold and it seemed ages since she had felt her benumbed fingers and toes. Even her face felt frozen. Her nose had developed a constant drip. If she didn't do something soon, she was going to find herself with pneumonia.

Unfortunately, her bedraggled state didn't exactly lend her the appearance of someone who had any business walking in the door of this particular apartment house. Eventually Teagan persuaded the doorman, not the one from the other night, to at least buzz the gentleman in the penthouse and ask him if he remembered a Teagan. And then, remembering she had never given him her name, she added that she was the street girl who had done him a favor several weeks back. The doorman could make of that message whatever he would.

It was clear by his disapproving expression he did. Even more obvious was his bafflement on returning a few seconds later to admit her. She found her way to the glass elevator with no difficulty. It was one of the details from that weird night that was indelibly etched in her memory. She would need to get some of those memories out of her head if she was going to go through with her plan. She gave her reflection in the elevator doors a quick examination. Normally the roughness of her life left her little opportunity for feminine vanity. She was too busy focusing on keeping alive to spare any concern for what she looked like. Remembering the elegance of the penthouse, however, she did regret the mess confronting her gaze.

Her hair was worse than wind-tossed, having gone

unwashed ever since she had run out of hotel money. Her cheeks were pink and roughed by wind and weather; her skin chapped from constant exposure to the elements. The wool coat, which had seemed so warm and practical when she bought it, now looked stained and hideous after the few weeks it had spent out in the wet and mud. She didn't look like someone a man like Sir would toss a fiver to on the street, let alone allow to set her dirty feet into his penthouse.

It was while she was despairing over her appearance and her chances of carrying out her plan that the elevator came to a sudden stop and the doors opened. It was like that other night all over again. As she stepped slowly off the elevator and let the doors close behind her, she was again hemmed in by elegant finery and richness that took her breath away, even as it stirred a faint twinge of envy that one man should possess so much while people like her lived every day wondering where their next meal was coming from.

"So it is you," a low masculine voice observed from across the room. Sir was seated on one of the white leather armchairs, looking as dark and formidable as she remembered him, for all his casual tone. He was surrounded by stacks of papers and held a highlighter in one hand. But he set his work aside to regard her with an expression of expectancy. If he was curious as to what motive had brought her to him uninvited, he didn't show it, maintaining the sense Teagan remembered in him so well—that attitude of already knowing what was to come.

She studied him with a sort of horrified fascination.

Dressed in a white button-up shirt and black slacks, as if he had just come from somewhere important, he didn't look like a man capable of the scene she remembered so vividly from their last meeting. With his expression casual and his hair slicked into place, he looked cool and controlled and…yes, extremely attractive, in a vaguely sinister way. Or maybe it was just Teagan's previous experience evoking that indefinable sense of danger hovering around him. His expression remained bland as he surveyed her standing at the elevator doors, but she thought his calculating eyes were mocking her, even as they summed up her bedraggled condition.

"You can come closer," he said generously, apparently noting her reluctance to abandon her safe position for flight. "I don't bite."

Teagan didn't wholly believe that. She moved just far enough toward him they wouldn't have to raise their voices to converse but maintained enough distance to make a hasty retreat if the need arose.

His amused glance told her he noted her response, but he said nothing of it. Teagan read the silent confidence in his eyes that was an echo of her own uneasy thoughts. She looked away from his taunting gaze and concentrated on her purpose. If she let thoughts like these keep intruding on her determination, she may as well cast everything aside and make a hasty break toward safety right now.

Only it wasn't safety that lay on the other side of those elevator doors. It was another hungry night sleeping in an alley or under a hedgerow in some park. She wasn't sure she'd survive another night in the cold. This morning she had been alarmed at how difficult it was to get up when crawling from beneath a layer of snow. She'd been forced to keep moving all day, afraid of what would happen if she allowed herself to drop off into the seductive embrace of sleep for even a few minutes.

All these thoughts provided ample reason for her to hold her ground now. Nevertheless, despite her resolve, she leaped like a startled rabbit when he abruptly broke the silence. "Since you don't seem eager to explain your business, I assume you're waiting for me to ask. To what do I owe the pleasure of this charming and unexpected visit?"

Time to practice the speech she'd been working on all day. Teagan licked her lips and grasped after the planned speech as it scattered in bits from her memory. She was unused to such positions as the one she now found herself in. She had never considered herself stupid or socially awkward, but somehow he had the power to freeze her body and mind simply by looking at her. She stood floundering, trying to remember exactly what it was that had brought her here.

Taking an unexpected pity on her, he said, "If sitting down would help to loosen your tongue, you can pull up a seat." He indicated a leather armchair opposite him.

Teagan sensed he removed his eyes from her as a sort of concession, to give her a moment to compose herself again. Maybe he wasn't accustomed to women who flustered so easily. Perhaps it wasn't intentional; his brazen air of assurance, his mocking eyes, and the way his well-fitted shirt strained around his impressively muscled shoulders as he moved...

Where had that thought come from?

Teagan shook her head and fixed her concentration on something safe and ordinary: the fat, white chair settled opposite Sir. She walked to the seat with casual ease and displayed an unprecedented level of courage as she sank into it. So far so good, she reassured herself, as the thick leather upholstered cushions rose up to meet her. Still avoiding the eyes of her companion, she leaned back and crossed her legs. That immediately felt stupid. She wasn't putting a pair of long, elegant legs on display, after all. She was outfitted in torn, stained jeans, along with the several-sizes-too-large pair of men's tennis shoes she'd recently dug from a trash can.

Sir made a light throat clearing noise, reminding her he sat waiting. His attention was already half turned to the stack of papers he had set aside on her entrance. Clearly, he had other things to be doing.

"I'm, uh, sorry I caught you while you were busy," Teagan managed to say and then instantly gave herself a mental kick for departing from her planned script. This wasn't going well.

"It's nothing," he said dismissively. "Some business accounts. They'll wait."

Teagan nodded awkwardly. She hadn't intended to say anything at that moment, but suddenly, of its own accord, her mouth opened and the nervous statement spilled forth. "Sir, I'm here to blackmail you."

Chapter 7

TEAGAN ACTUALLY HEARD THE CLICK of her teeth as she clamped her mouth shut. She didn't know where the abrupt declaration had come from. Certainly in none of her mental rehearsals for this moment had she used the word blackmail. And yet now that she had committed herself to the statement, she had to admit it described adequately what she had in mind. She nodded and decided to stick with it.

Clinging to a strangely cool tone that sounded nothing like her usual voice she plowed onward, sealing whatever fate waited ahead. "That's right. You heard me," she said evenly into the stunned silence. It was the first time she'd ever had the pleasure of seeing Sir at a loss and suspecting it might be the last, she meant to take all the enjoyment from it she could.

She continued. "Those five hundred dollars you passed over to me last month were just pennies to you. Don't think I'm so stupid I didn't see that. From the moment I saw where and how you lived I knew you were worth much, much more. And yet because you viewed me as ignorant trash off the street you saw no reason to offer me fair pay." She didn't know where she was getting the courage to voice such thoughts. But these feelings of injustice had been growing in her since she had set foot into this place.

Sir didn't take long to recover from what must have been a surprising onslaught. "Fair pay?" he repeated her words softly as if weighing them. "You feel you were granted inadequate compensation for the tasks you carried out?"

"If 'inadequate compensation' is Latin for 'not enough money', that's right," Teagan said, her hopes rising. At least he seemed to be giving the matter thought.

Her optimism, as it turned out, was premature. Not until he spoke again did she recognize the telltale flash deep within his brown eyes. "So you feel you might have earned better money elsewhere that night," he said.

"Well, I—"

But he didn't let her finish. "Or maybe it's just that the duties you carried out were so difficult or required such a level of skill no one but you could have met them?"

He was turning her argument on its head. Teagan decided it was time she wrested back control of the conversation. "I'm not saying I was the only person for the job," she put in defensively. "Only that you could afford to give more, and that I..." She stumbled a little under his gaze. "I...deserve more," she finished lamely, her voice dropping to a mumble.

He surprised her by seemingly shifting the topic. "Do you know why I picked you for the job that night?" he asked. He answered his own question. "Evidently not. I was walking down the street, on my way home from the office, enjoying the evening air on my lonely stroll. And then I passed by a darkened alleyway, where I discovered a miserable specimen of humanity huddled on the filthy ground, beneath a pile of rags. Moved by the horrible conditions I saw this sad creature suffering under, I made up my mind on a whim to offer her first chance at a task I needed fulfilled." He spoke the explanation with no hint of sentiment so that his implied sympathy was hard to swallow.

Teagan bristled at the implication he had approached her out of pity. She countered with, "You know, most people who want to help just throw me a ten dollar bill."

"Did you want a ten dollar bill?" he shot back easily. "Because I thought your argument was that I didn't pay enough."

He had trapped Teagan neatly with his logic, and although she knew there had to be a way around his twisting of the argument, she wasn't quick-witted enough to work it out.

He appeared to take satisfaction in her confusion. "And now," he continued, "after already receiving more than your due, you have the unmitigated nerve to come prowling around here again, begging for another handout."

"I wasn't begging." Teagan's head snapped up. For an instant she felt too insulted to care about the plan or anything else. "I have never begged for anything in my life," she said hotly. "And I hope I'd die before I asked any favors of you. After that night—" She broke off abruptly. This was the first time either of them had made open reference to what had passed between them before.

"Ah, so now we get to the real root of your visit." He said it coolly, but his eyes sparked with some unreadable emotion. "Is this a question of revenge then? Have you stormed back in self-righteous indignation to make the coldhearted villain pay?"

There was such sarcasm to his tone that if Teagan had harbored any doubts about how he really saw her, they were dispelled. She was right when she'd accused him of thinking of her as street trash. The offense she felt made it easy to form her next reply. "This isn't a matter of revenge, Sir. Just a question of whether or not I've received the payment due me."

But he wasn't to be silenced so easily. She thought he was beginning to enjoy decimating her arguments. He leaned back in his seat, elbows resting on the armrests of his chair and fingers templed in a thoughtful gesture. "So you still think you want to discuss payment, do you? I thought we'd already exhausted the topic and moved on. However, if I've left any doubts in your mind, let me close the subject more fully." His expression became direct. "You won't be seeing another penny."

"But—"

He forestalled her protests. "We agreed on a sum. I paid you the amount, despite the fact you rightfully forfeited it when you broke my rules by opening the silver box."

"But the box was empty," Teagan finally had a chance to put in.

He regarded her shrewdly. "And was the refrigerator also empty when you helped yourself to its contents?"

Teagan was left speechless. How could he know of that?

He dismissed the explanation he apparently expected with a wave of one hand. It was just as well. Teagan had no excuses prepared. "Never mind that," he said. "I can afford to lose a few pieces of fruit. I even gave you your precious money, despite your light fingers. I think you must admit that was more than generous on my part. You can count it as reparation for any unnerving behavior I may have indulged in that night. I was not myself."

May have indulged in? There was no question his behavior had been more than unnerving, Teagan fumed. Surely he saw as much, whether he was willing to admit it or not. Anger granted her greater courage. "Reparation?" she demanded, rising from her chair. "Do you think I would take money as some sort of payoff for a thing like that?"

"And yet," he said coolly from his seat, "that was exactly what you had in mind when you came here, wasn't it? As if I could have been harmed by your blabbing nonsense about some ridiculous little incident all over town." Again he cut off the protest she was about to offer. "Let's look at the facts as anyone else would, shall we?"

He held up a large hand that Teagan couldn't help noticing flashed a ring on nearly every finger. It was yet another reminder of his careless wealth. Either unaware or uninterested in her private thoughts, he began ticking off the facts on his fingers.

"To begin with, what evidence do you have of any wrongdoing on my part? None but the words of your own mouth. Not a very trustworthy source in most eyes."

Teagan's cheeks grew warm in the way they did when she was truly angry. "That's not—"

"Not fair, I agree," he admitted. "But it remains a fact." He ticked off his first finger and moved on to a second. "Next, what can you honestly say happened? A stranger threatened you. Is that all you've got? Worse crimes are committed every night on the streets of this city. What are they going to do—throw me in jail?"

This time Teagan couldn't keep silent. "A threat?" she asked incredulously. "Is that what you call it? You terrified me. You hurt me. I had bruises that took days to heal." She was startled to find her voice shaking, but she couldn't seem to gain control of it. "I was afraid out of my mind. I thought you were going to murder me and stuff my body into some dumpster…"

Her voice broke off, which was probably just as well. Her words had dropped to a whisper, and she found herself trembling as the frightening scene replayed in her head. She had never before felt so close to death as she had that night. The strange fierceness that had possessed him… She became abruptly aware of the silence around her—of the emptiness of this room that held only two lonely inhabitants. As fear began to tickle against the back of her mind, she asked herself what she had been thinking to return here.

Sir appeared unaware of the new turn of her thoughts. He held his silence so long Teagan almost dared to imagine her words might have stirred some pangs of remorse in him.

"I…didn't realize the incident had affected you so deeply," he said. There was no apology in his words— no sympathy. He merely eyed her as if trying to work out some sort of foreign puzzle.

"Is that all you have to say?" she whispered disbelievingly. "No apology—no explanation?"

He shrugged. "Why should I beg forgiveness for your overactive imagination? I didn't do what you feared. I probably wouldn't have even—"

"Probably?" Teagan had heard enough. "That does it. I've been reasonable. I've given you every chance to make up for…everything. Well, forget it. I don't want your money anymore. All I want now is to spread this story to every ear within hearing distance. We'll see how well your respectability and your reputation can stand up to the light of day. I'll tell how you handled me—I'll tell about your weird rituals with the music and the locked room and the place settings for secret guests who never arrive—"

Seeing the shadow pass over his face, she broke off quickly. It wasn't the charge of his rough treatment that had brought about the change in him. It was as she spoke of the secret rituals that the look of mild annoyance he'd been wearing swiftly faded from his features to be replaced by another, sharper look. Teagan knew that expression. It held something of the fierce attitude that had overtaken him the other night. But there was also a colder, more controlled façade stretched tightly over his fury that somehow made him seem all the more dangerous.

"Is that the real threat then?" he asked, his voice tense, his eyes boring twin holes into her. "You expected me to pay to keep you quiet about my *rituals*?"

As he spoke, he rose and took a step toward her. Teagan found herself retreating an equal distance. The barely restrained anger in his tone brought back an unpleasant taste of the panic she had known once before in his presence. Teagan opened her mouth to take back her threat—to promise to keep his secrets—but no sound escaped her dry throat.

He continued to advance on her until Teagan found herself backing into a solid wall in her efforts to keep out of his reach.

"You enjoy examining things—prying into areas that are none of your business," he continued, crowding her against the wall. "Take a look around you now," he invited. "What do you see?"

Teagan was already casting wild glances around her, looking for some avenue of escape. All that met her search was an empty apartment with just one way in and one way out.

"That's right," he said, seemingly reading her

thoughts. "It's just you and me. If I am the evil, loathsome excuse for a human being you imagined me that night, what's to prevent me from permanently silencing a foolish little street girl who threatens to shoot her mouth off about secrets I don't care to have divulged to the public?"

Teagan swallowed, unsure what answer she should give even if she were in a mental condition to form a rational response. Right now, she would have said about anything he wanted to hear just to get out of this place alive. Her heartbeat was thundering so loudly in her ears his voice seemed to filter in from a distance.

His face was now so near that the words he whispered were a breath against her skin. "What," he asked slowly, deliberately, "is to prevent your fears from becoming reality?" His fathomless dark eyes were intense, taunting, angry... How could they be so many things at once? She flinched as he abruptly raised one hand to touch the hollow of her throat. His hand was warm—gentle—as he stroked a careful finger across her skin. But the dangerous glint in his eyes and the hint of underlying anger in his tone didn't match the lightness of his touch.

Teagan had the horrible sense that at any moment his mockingly gentle touch was going to grow firmer. How easy would it be for her fears to come true—for him to tighten his hands around her throat, squeeze the life out of her, and then discard her lifeless body in the shadows of some back alley? Surely such an act would be easy for a man like him. He had his wealth and reputation to protect him. Besides that, he had already demonstrated he was powerful enough to carry out the deed. The gleam of sadistic pleasure in his eyes as he contemplated her fearful state made it obvious he possessed the cruelty for such an act.

Teagan became aware of an odd, surging motion in the floor beneath her feet. Was it the floor moving or her shaky limbs that made it suddenly difficult for her to maintain her stance? Her lungs ached and she realized abruptly it was because she was holding her breath. The room behind Sir grew hazy. Even Sir's face was now difficult to focus on and she gave up the effort, closing her eyes. She felt his strong hands wrapping around her waist but whether he put them there to hold her in place or to prevent her collapsing, it was impossible to know. The last thing she consciously thought of before falling into oblivion was how desperately she regretted returning to this place and this man.

Chapter 8

W HEN TEAGAN AWOKE SHE HAD no idea where she was. She was lying prone on her back and her head felt light, as if she were coming out of a long sleep. Opening her eyes, she expected to see the bright blue of a winter sky overhead with the towering shadows of city skyscrapers etched across its face. Instead, dim indoor lighting revealed unfamiliar surroundings. The walls above her were red brick and the ceiling high. A black wrought iron candelabra hung suspended over her head.

Slowly, cautiously, Teagan lifted herself enough to look around. The careful movement sent the world spinning dizzyingly before her eyes for a moment, and she had to concentrate on a single spot on the opposite side of the room until the feeling subsided. Her visual point was a square, black frame fixed onto the far wall. The frame held a large picture that looked something like a newspaper clipping, featuring two men in suits sharing a handshake. Even at this distance Teagan recognized the face of one of them. Sir...

That recognition sent her spiraling into a descent of panic as events came crashing back to mind. Her return to Sir's apartment, the tense confrontation, his threats… She shot bolt upright, scanning the room for another presence. To her vast relief, she seemed to be alone. She had feared to find him hovering nearby, watching. The brief rush of relief she felt was short lived. Whether Sir was presently here or not, there seemed no question he must be somewhere close by. The luxuriousness of her surroundings told her she was still in the apartment.

She supposed that was something to be grateful for—that she had not as yet been deposited into the much feared dumpster or even dropped into the river. And yet there was nothing to say she was beyond the danger line. In fact, the position she now found herself in was almost as alarming as her last memories of Sir looming over her. She was sitting in a red-blanketed bed with a massive headboard and footboard towering at either end, its thick posts stretching almost to the ceiling. At one end of the large room stood an upright chest of drawers, and beside it, a tall armoire. There were heavy matching nightstands on both sides of the bed, and an oak bookshelf with glass panes lining an entire wall.

All of this Teagan took in with a hurried glance, the bulk of her attention being reserved for what she really sought: a way out. There were three wooden doors in the room: one in the far wall and the other two on either side of the armoire. Scrambling from beneath the soft comforter, Teagan slipped out of the massively carved bed with a feeling akin to that of a lobster escaping the pot. The floor beneath her still-in-place tennis shoes was gray-tiled with scarlet colored rugs scattered here and there. She half-tiptoed, half-ran to the door in the far wall, unable to make up her mind which was the more important just now, stealth or speed.

She gripped the thick steel handle, and turning it down, gave the door a tug. Nothing happened. She tried again, but still the door stayed stuck fast. With a sinking sensation, Teagan realized it was locked from the outside. Not prepared to give up yet, she next tried the other doors near the armoire. One turned out to be a deep walk-in closet with shelves and racks enough to hold an entire department store full of clothes. Most of them were stuffed too.

The other door let into the roomiest bathroom she had ever seen, featuring an immense tiled tub and a long granite topped counter with two clear glass sinks and dozens of drawers. The floor was tiled and the rugs, towels, and shower curtain continued the theme of scarlet and black. In the corner near the tub, a small stone fountain beside a potted plant provided a soft trickling noise. A long settee along another wall gave the room more the atmosphere of a place meant to lounge in than to carry out the bodily necessities.

An immense round metal-framed mirror hung over the bathroom countertop, looking as if its impressive weight should have dragged it right down from the wall. Teagan hardly recognized her own reflection gazing out of it. Her face was pale, her eyes wide, and she had a wary expression, as if expecting something horrible to leap out in front of her at any moment. She hesitated long enough to run her fingers through her dark hair in a useless attempt to tame the wild tresses. Something about her elegant surroundings made her do that.

She reentered the bedroom and told herself she had come to the end of her fruitless search. There was no other way in or out. This room lacked even a window, although it would have done her no good anyway this high above the ground. As she scanned the room with a sinking feeling of despair, her gaze returned to the framed picture she had first noticed on waking. It was a newspaper clipping. Curiosity made her move closer to study the two men photographed. The one was definitely Sir, but she didn't recognize the second man. There was a small caption beneath the picture. It read:

J. Rotham of NationBank closes deal with board of directors.

Suddenly, Teagan knew two things about Sir she hadn't known before—his identity and his occupation. Unless the other man photographed was Mr. J. Rotham. Somehow she doubted it. Sir struck her as being too vain to display monuments to other people on his walls. Unfortunately, Teagan could see no way either bit of information would be of use to her until she got out of this place.

Nevertheless, appetite whetted by her first discovery, she looked around the room with a new eye. Hadn't she been full of questions about Sir and his psycho behavior? It seemed she was in the right place to learn some answers if she could only set aside her fears long enough to do some exploration. She might even find something of use here—maybe a weapon she could use to defend herself if he returned. Didn't all rich businessmen sleep with pistols under their beds so they could shoot themselves when their businesses went bankrupt? A quick peek under the ruffled bed skirt revealed that one, at least, did not.

Teagan moved on to the tall armoire. She felt a little uneasy opening its heavy doors, as if Sir might somehow sense his things being rifled through and come swooping out of nowhere to stop her. Nothing of the sort happened, of course, and the armoire held nothing but more clothing, neatly pressed suits in every variation of the colors black and gray. As if he didn't have enough of those in the closet. There were even a couple of tuxes, complete with shiny black shoes to accompany them. And ties, dozens of those.

Teagan swung the armoire doors closed and went on to examine a neighboring set of shelves built into one corner of the room. She cast only a brief glance over the titles. Books on business, personal finance, self-help books... She would never have pegged Sir as a man who needed a book to teach him how to operate a computer but apparently he did. He also seemed to have a surprising interest in medicine and science. There were a lot of those books on his shelf too.

For fiction his tastes were less varied—and surprisingly nerdy. An entire half of the shelf was devoted to fantastic novels of vampires, werewolves, ghosts, and the undead. It seemed odd to think of a man like Sir sitting back in the evenings to crack open the covers of books with names like *Blood Dawn*, *Chill of Death*, and *Under the Full Moon*.

But his reading tastes didn't tell her much about him. She moved on to a nearby chest of drawers. The first few drawers were nothing but socks and underwear. No interesting discoveries there.

It was in one of the bottom drawers that she stumbled across an unexpected discovery. This space was filled with odd articles of winter time clothing: gloves, scarves, and thick woolen socks. Teagan almost closed the drawer, but at the last moment she caught sight of something out of place. There nestled among the other things was a thin white envelope. Why would such a thing be kept with his winter accessories unless he had placed it there to hide it?

Snatching up the envelope, she studied the outside. It was addressed to Mr. J. Rotham of NationBank and had a return address in Vermont. The postmark told her it had been mailed three months ago. That was about all her amateur detective work could tell her without looking inside. Luckily the top had already been slit and she had only to tilt the envelope upside down for its contents to come sliding out. It held a folded letter on plain, cheap paper.

Unfolding the note, Teagan found the message inside was so messily scrawled it was hardly legible. With effort, she made out some of the lines. They all seemed to be angry rants and threats against Sir for foreclosing a loan on a failing business—Glintwood

Options. There was no explanation of what sort of business this Glintwood Options was, but the letter's writer made frequent references to groundbreaking discoveries and amazing advancements to benefit the human state, all of which would now be halted due to the actions of Mr. J. Rotham.

The letter closed with an ominous hint of revenge that would have left Teagan feeling deeply uneasy had she been the recipient of such threats. Had it made Sir uneasy? That would explain his hiding the letter away. Teagan privately thought in his place, she would have felt more comfortable tossing it into the fireplace than slipping it into a drawer only a few feet away from her bed. Who needed the constant reminder of an unnerving exchange with such an unpleasant man? Then again Sir's own moods could be black enough, maybe he regarded the note as more of an amusing curiosity than an object of disturbance.

She flipped the envelope over and studied the return address again. There'd been no signature in the letter but there was a name here—Dr. Mortimer Green. "Sixteen hundred Old Pine Road, River Falls, Vermont," she read aloud, committing the address to memory. One never knew when this sort of information could come in handy. A subtle idea was already nudging at the back of her mind about how she might turn this Dr. Green's desire for vengeance against Sir to her advantage. If she got out of here alive, that was.

It was as she formed this very thought that she became aware of a soft rattling of the handle on the door leading out of the bedroom. There was a faint clinking noise, like that of a lock being turned, and then the door was creaking open. Teagan shoved the letter and its envelope back into the bottom dresser drawer and slammed the drawer closed not a second too soon.

Chapter 9

THE DOOR SWUNG OPEN AND in stepped Sir. Expressionlessly, he took in her position. Teagan backed away from the dresser, trying to move casually but feeling as if all the focus of the room somehow pointed toward the hastily closed drawer. Why was he looking at it like that? Had she left it open a crack? Was a sock or something dangling out? It took an extraordinary effort not to cast a guilty glance that direction. She eyed the room's single passage of escape, already vanishing behind Sir's back as he swung the door shut behind him.

As he moved further into the room, Teagan took a step backward but he only walked around the space, inspecting its contents as if expecting to find something tampered with or missing. It seemed a colossally arrogant gesture for someone who had just acted as he had to now be concerned about her stealing his things... Teagan almost forgot she had in fact been guilty of both meddling and stealing in this place. Never mind, she told herself. She'd had her reasons.

The memory of that prompted her to exhibit a level of courage she didn't truly feel. She broke the silence by saying, "I hope you won't think I'm prying if I ask just what fate you have in mind for me and how long you plan on keeping me here."

For the first time he switched his attention from their surroundings to look directly at her. Teagan was careful not to meet his eyes. In the past, that had proved a dangerous thing to do.

"Keeping you here?" he repeated. "I'm sure I hadn't thought of doing anything of the kind. I don't know whether or not you've noticed…" His tone was ironic. "But this place happens to be my bedroom. And while you're fairly pretty and lively enough company, I think we'd be a bit crowded over time. Besides I'm not comfortable with strangers rifling through my belongings or helping themselves to any shiny little valuables they happen to pick up."

Teagan was still too unnerved by the last scene between them to fall into the trap of his easy conversation now. "Don't try to pretend I'm anything less than a prisoner here. Why else would you have brought me to this room and locked me in?"

"Locked?" He feigned confusion. "I don't know what you mean. The door opened perfectly easily for me. But I apologize if you felt yourself for one moment—how did you put it—a prisoner?"

Teagan was finally working up enough nerve to insert her own note of sarcasm as she said, "If I was always free to go at any time then explain to me what I'm doing here."

He shrugged. "You took some sudden spell as silly girls often do and fainted dead away in my living room floor. Would you have preferred I let you lie there?"

Teagan didn't buy his explanation for a moment and kept a guarded watch on him as he circled around the room. He paused before the dresser and eyed the bottom drawer. Was it her imagination or was there a tiny scrap of white showing over its edge?

He continued with, "You know for a young woman who lives alone on the city streets you appear to have an unusually fanciful imagination. How old are you anyway? Eighteen? Nineteen?"

As he spoke he crouched on one knee before the drawer. Teagan's attention was so wrapped up in what he was doing she forgot herself enough to give information she wouldn't normally have shared with this man. "Twenty-two," she admitted, nervously watching him slide the drawer open to free the white envelope that had been caught over its edge.

"Hmmm," he said, handling the envelope. "I wouldn't have thought it. Surely a woman of your age knows better than to pry into others' things—or at least not to get caught if she does."

He replaced the envelope over a pile of socks and slid the drawer shut again. Teagan thought he would say something more about her infraction or concerning the contents of the letter but he surprised her by changing the subject entirely. "I've been giving some thought to the proposition you made earlier," he said, facing her suddenly.

"Prop—proposition?" Teagan couldn't think

what he was talking about. The only concern on her mind right now was how quickly she could get out of here before he took on another of his unpredictable, sadistic moods.

"Yes. The one about my paying you a sum of money to keep my secrets secret." A faint smile hovered around the corner of his lips. "Although you were being overly dramatic when you formed your ridiculous threats about exposing certain of my personal actions to the public, it's true I'm a man who values my privacy in all things. I would as soon my 'rituals,' as you call them, didn't become the talk of the town. People wouldn't understand."

Teagan didn't understand. However all she said was, "I won't tell. I won't speak a word of anything I heard or saw here. I promise if you'll just…"

"Just let you go?" he finished. "But I've already told you you're free to come or go as you please whenever the notion strikes you. It's wild ideas like this talk being locked up that make you seem immature beneath your years."

He could call her immature. He could call her anything he liked for all she cared, so long as he meant the part about allowing her to leave. She was still half convinced he had some ominous plan of silencing her permanently. While she had to fear that, her chief thoughts were on beating a hasty escape as soon as possible. To that end, she headed for the door.

Anticipating her action, he moved to block her exit.

"You said I was free. You said I could go." Teagan didn't care if she babbled or if there was a panicky note to her protests. "I've told you I won't speak to a soul about—"

"Ah, but you see that's where we both know you're lying," he interrupted. "With an imagination and a curiosity like yours, you're not capable of keeping a secret for the space of an hour out of my sight. Not for anything as paltry as a mere promise anyway." His tone sharpened. "That's why I've devised a much better way of keeping you quiet."

Teagan's eyes widened as he stepped nearer.

"Money," he said softly. "That's the one thing that will keep your greedy little heart satisfied. It's the one thing that could buy your silence. I don't mean to take you up on your exact offer, of course. That would be more than you deserve, and besides, such an easy flow of cash would only make you greedier. You'd be returning to me again and again as long as I kept opening my wallet for you and the day I stopped doing that, you'd betray me." His expression grew dark. "If there's one thing I despise it's a blackmailer."

Teagan shivered at his tone. "Then what are you suggesting?" Some inner part of her was shocked at the question—shocked she could care about money at a frightening time like this. But another deeper part of her was pricking up its ears with interest. He had been right in his assessment of her. The hint of money was probably the only thing that could have stirred her from her fearful state just now.

His expression said he had noted this. "My plan is to give you a chance to earn your money," he said. "I think you already know how."

Teagan bit her lip. "The rituals?" she asked uneasily.

He smiled humorlessly. "If you want to call them that, yes. It's a chore I'll need performed again from time to time and you've proven you're capable of carrying it off well enough. Learn to obey my instructions more thoroughly the next time around and I don't think we'll have any more unpleasant incidents like the last. What do you say?"

Teagan swallowed. "Will you be here on those occasions?"

He asked, "Would you come if I were?"

"No."

"Then I won't be."

She was astonished at herself for even considering the idea. Twice before need had forced her to voluntarily step into this man's lair and both times she had regretted it. Only a few minutes ago she had been thinking she'd do anything just to escape this place. Apparently experience hadn't made her any wiser. The suggestion of money was about to draw her again into the very trap she dreaded.

She voiced none of these thoughts aloud however. When she opened her mouth it was to say, "I'll take the job—but only on the condition I am never to see you in person. I'll come here at the times you designate. You can leave me my money and any instructions in a note. But I don't ever want to bump into you while I'm here. You—you kind of creep me out a little."

She didn't care whether he found that last admission amusing or not. The whole deal would hinge on his response. She'd had enough of his weird moods and the scenes he created with them. No price was worth putting herself through any more of these unnerving experiences.

Luckily, he seemed undisturbed by her insistence. "I think we have ourselves an understanding," he said.

"Not so fast. We haven't discussed some details yet. Just how often am I supposed to come here?"

"As often as I ask it," he said simply. His tone made it clear she wasn't going to get any further answer on that.

"All right. Fair enough," she said. "But if I'm going to be kept at your constant beck and call I expect to be well paid for it. The pocket change you gave me last time didn't see me through a week. I know you're worth plenty more."

"What I'm worth," he said, "is none of your concern. If I'm going to employ you, I want it clear it's you who work for me. I'll be setting the amount, and you can take it or not."

He didn't make her ask again but named a monthly sum so large Teagan at first thought she was mishearing. "Is that—is that dollars or cents?" she asked incredulously.

He smirked. "Dollars. I'll eventually arrange a regular payment system, but for now I'll give you a portion of next month's payment in advance. Obviously you need it." His gaze swept up and down her skinny figure and grungy clothing.

Teagan wouldn't let herself be rattled. He could insult her all he liked at this point. The kind of money he was talking could float her for weeks if she was careful. She could get herself an apartment, get off the streets… Suddenly she saw possibilities she hadn't imagined could be open to someone like her. Just to have a dry roof over her head would be a relief. There was just one glitch in the whole system.

"How permanent is this job going to be?" she asked.

She had the sense somehow that he was disturbed by the question. "The length of time is indefinite."

Indefinite. Then she'd better be squirreling something away every month to live from when this job fell through. "I just have one more question," she said.

He smiled. "Somehow I think with you it will always be one more question."

She ignored that. "Why is it you're willing to pay someone like me so much to do this simple work for you? I mean, you put on some music, lock a door, and set the table for dinner. Why can't you do those things for yourself?"

His expression was closed. "You can consider the generous payment a tip for not asking too many questions."

"I see," she said. "Then I guess the only thing left to ask is, when do I start?"

Chapter 10

TEAGAN'S PROJECT FOR THE NEXT day was to find a suitable apartment to lay her head at night—one cheap enough she could make Sir's cash stretch from one month to the next with still a little left over for other needs. The place she finally settled on was a tiny room on the first floor of a crumbling apartment house. It was crammed directly beneath a stairwell so she would have to listen to the echoing clank of people's feet stomping up and down the stairs all day.

Rather than a set of rooms, it was a single living-sleeping area with peeling olive wallpaper and a stained toilet set out openly in one corner of the room. But there was at least a thin curtain partitioning the toilet and shower off from the rest of the space, and some fairly sturdy pieces of furniture that came with the room. Teagan doubted someone spoiled to luxury like Sir would have thought this dingy little hole worth living in, with its crumbling ceiling plaster and broken light fixture. But to Teagan it was a sanctuary—a place where she was afforded a level of safety and privacy she hadn't known in a long time. What was more important was that her rent here would be low enough to allow her to put some money back.

As she sat on the edge of the creaky bed and surveyed her new home, Teagan felt a faint stirring of hope within her. It didn't look like much, but this little room was going to be the start of a new life for her. She was going to keep a job, live under a roof, and eat regular meals like everybody else. No more sleeping along curbs and huddling under cardboard boxes to keep off the rain and the drifting snow.

She decided a good way to kick off her new, civilized existence was to take a bath. Stripping off her mud-encrusted coat and grubby jeans and shirt, she wrinkled her nose at the strong odor emanating from her unwashed body. She couldn't recall the last time she'd bathed, unless she counted soaking up rainwater as washing. The room's last inhabitant—an elderly lady in her seventies, Teagan had been told—had left the shriveled remnants of a bar of rock hard soap in a dish atop the battered sink. Lacking anything better, she snatched this up as she stepped into the plastic shower.

She tried to persuade herself the weird, orange stains underfoot were just rust marks from the metal pipes overhead. When she turned the single handle in the wall the showerhead sputtered a moment before blasting out a stream of icy water over her. It took a moment for the water to warm up, but when it did Teagan worked what lather she could out of the dried bar of soap and concentrated her efforts on her hair. Shampoo and washcloths were something she would have to pick up at a later time. The noisy pipes over the shower leaked a little, spraying sprinkles of rust-colored water over the floor, but that too was a problem for another day.

When at last she had sluiced all the filth she could from her skin and rinsed her hair thoroughly, she twisted the shower handle hard to stop the last continuing dribble from the spigot and toweled herself off with a musty blanket from the bed. There was nothing else handy. With no hairbrush lying around, she combed her long hair out as best she could with her fingers, standing before a cracked mirror hanging over the back of the front door.

She had no clean clothes to change into so she wrapped herself again in the old blanket before sitting on the bed to plan her next move. Sooner or later she was going to have to wash out her dirty clothes, hang them up from the ceiling fan to dry, and then drag them back on to wear to the nearest cheap department store. She would need to buy new clothes—particularly new underwear. Also, she needed soap, towels, food, and eating utensils to stock the cabinets with. The room came with a broken oven and a minifridge but it might be good to own a microwave.

She felt exhausted just thinking of all she needed to buy. Already in her mind's eye she saw that pile of cash from Sir shrinking as she delved into it again and again. She lay back on the bed for a brief rest and found herself instead drifting off to sleep.

Teagan didn't waste her time in the sort of fancy shops where she knew the clerks would look askance at her poor appearance and worn clothing. She didn't have that kind of money to spend anyway. Sir had been generous but not that generous. So she concentrated on the kinds of places where she could afford to shop—consignment stores for the most part. But no one said just because your clothes were used they had to be ratty. She picked up some cute clothing she hoped had a trendy, vintage look to it—or possibly it just looked old. Either way, by the time she left the second store she was weighted down with bags. She also had significantly less money, but she wouldn't think of that just yet.

Now it was time she interrupted her shopping trip to deal with one important arrangement. She was unsure whether it was the winter chill or some warning sense of premonition that caused a cold wave to wash over her as she stepped into the nearest post office. The halls branching from the front entrance were long and shadowed, and even though strangers milled all around her, Teagan had the frightening sense of being utterly alone as she proceeded to the row of clerk's desks in the distance. The voices and footsteps of the men and women rushing past on their busy errands seemed to echo up to the ceiling. Teagan did her best to ignore the chunk of ice that had settled in her belly as she thought of what she was about to do.

Gripping the handles of her shopping bags with suddenly cold hands, she made her way to the nearest counter. Dropping the bags to the floor, she told the dour faced man behind it she wanted to rent a post office box. It wasn't until the necessary forms had been filled that she remembered she lacked the implements she needed to finish her task.

"Um, do you have a pen and paper?" she sheepishly asked the clerk. "I need to write a letter. Like, right now."

He had already turned away. "Ma'am, you can buy stationary products at the corner drugstore."

"I'm sorry, I know that, but I really need this to go out today. It's urgent, and I'm afraid if I leave and come back later…"

"All right, all right." His disapproving frown said he didn't consider her personal problems any concern of his, but she guessed he found it easier to comply with her request than to argue. "I have a notepad around here somewhere."

"Thank you so much." She put on her most grateful smile as he dug around beneath his counter and produced a pen and a yellow notepad.

She slid to the corner of the counter where she would be out of the way of the other customers and scooted her shopping bags along with her, before bending her head over the lined pad and starting to work. She bit her lip and tried to tune out the noise and motion going on around her, so that she could focus on what she needed to say.

> *Dr. Green,*
>
> *It has come to my attention that you and I share a mutual enemy. I haven't the time to go into the details of how I came to meet Mr. J. Rotham, or of how I happened to learn of the hatred between you. All I will say is that I share your dislike of the man. If I didn't, I wouldn't be making you this offer.*

Her pen paused in moving across the page as she hesitated. Did she really want to go through with this? Suppose Sir found out he was being double-crossed? Besides, she had no reason to suppose Dr. Green was still revenge thirsty, and even if he was, who was to say he was willing to go to these kinds of lengths to see his desire realized?

But then, as if to reassure her in her moment of wavering, snatches of the angry letter she had read from Dr. Green floated before her mind. Those hadn't been the threats of a man content to let his anger go. They were the words of a man who meant business. One who might be willing to pay generously to see that business conducted.

She returned to her work.

> *By a strange twist of fate, I have come to be in a trusted position close to this man we both have cause to despise. I will be blunt. My financial circumstances are difficult. If you have some plan for avenging yourself of Mr. Rotham and if somehow my own efforts could benefit this plan, I am ready and eager to take part in it. For a price, I will do anything you ask, will provide any information on*

this man or his movements you want. If my offer interests you, if there's any way we could come to a mutually beneficial agreement, you may respond to the below address.

She signed her name hastily, before she could change her mind, and printed the address of her new post office box at the bottom of the note. She had to buy a whole box of envelopes from the clerk before she could slip her letter into one, seal it, then scribble the address she had previously memorized across the front.

Back out on the sidewalk, she hunched her shoulders against the blast of the icy wind as she hurried away from what she imaginatively dubbed the scene off her crime. She shuddered to think what might happen if Sir were to find out what she had just done. But then, why should he, she asked herself. The man might be many things, but all seeing he wasn't.

Despite the dreariness of the day around her and the faint unease she still felt at what she had done, another more sensible part of her was relieved. With this new direction she'd taken, she need no longer rely solely on the good graces of a man she had little cause to trust.

She stopped by her room just long enough to drop off her bags and change into some of her new clothing. She took the crinkled roll of cash out of her pocket and put some of it into the new purse she had bought, stuffing the rest under the edge of a loose floor tile. In a neighborhood like this you didn't take chances, even if you were someone who appeared to have little to steal.

After that she was off again to purchase a whole avalanche of supplies. By the time her day had ended she had new sheets for the bed, new bathroom and kitchen necessities, and enough groceries to last her a week. She had even picked up a few personal supplies like a hairbrush and comb and a bottle of deodorant. She had no idea when she had last brushed her teeth, but she bought a toothbrush and tube of toothpaste too.

As she finally sat down to eat a macaroni dinner cooked in her new microwave, she thought to herself that at last she was set. She hadn't been so organized in ages. Now if she could only keep her job long enough to stay that way.

It was approaching dusk the next evening when Teagan stepped off the glass elevator and into the middle of Sir's living room. She could see the last glow of the fiery sun sinking down behind the skyscrapers in the distance. A glance at a digital clock on a low table told her she was exactly on time. She had just a few minutes until seven-thirty—the hour she had been instructed to begin her routine.

Hanging her purse on the coatrack—it still felt strange carrying the unfamiliar accessory—she slipped off her new waist-length jacket and went into the den to retrieve the key from beneath the silver box. She was growing accustomed to the lavishness of these rooms now, and dressed in her new clothing, no longer felt as dirty and out of place as she once had.

Her hair felt light and loose swishing around her shoulders as she moved. It hadn't been free of that waist-length braid in years. Earlier that afternoon she had visited a hair salon and had it cut and styled to a tidier length so it now fell in soft waves to just below her shoulder blades. She still couldn't help glancing at it admiringly every time she passed a mirror. The little square mirror set up atop Sir's desk in the den was no exception, and it was while studying her reflection she heard the pendulum clock on the mantel chime the half hour. There was no more time to be wasted.

It all felt familiar as she began the routine. Sir had left her a little note near the silver box with a list of instructions penned in what she thought was a rather ironic tone. She suspected he was mocking her rule against face-to-face meetings, but she didn't care. As long as he paid her on time and kept far away from the apartment while she was here, he could say or do anything he pleased. The note detailed her tasks in much the same way she had performed them last.

Setting it down, she slid the silver box aside and retrieved the hidden key. At least she felt no temptation this time to crack the ornate silver lid. She had been through that adventure before. Proceeding to the living room, she inserted the key in the latch of the study door, turned it, and slid it back out. She hardly even felt a twinge of curiosity this time about what lay on the other side of the door. After her good fortune in gaining this job it seemed foolish to look a gift horse in the mouth.

Returning the key to its usual hiding place, she started the CD player, which had already been cued, and moved on to the kitchen. The wine was stored in the same part of the refrigerator she remembered and everything she needed for the table's place setting was where it should be. It was only a matter of a few minutes to finish the arrangements and then she stood back studying her work. She wondered what all of this meant. Sir wasn't here to enjoy a meal, even had there been any food on his plate. No one but her was listening to the music blaring deafeningly out over the speakers. There wasn't even anyone here to know whether or not she had locked the study door. Was Sir really expecting some sort of late night guest to drop by, and if so who?

It occurred to her he might have a girlfriend. He had never spoken of one and she hadn't come across any photos of a woman during the time she had spent in his room yesterday, but then she hadn't exactly been looking for that sort of thing. For that matter, where did he go on these evening outings? He hadn't been here when she had arrived and, if his word held good, didn't meant to be here when she returned to undo all her work of tonight. Didn't he have to work in the mornings? Surely even a man with all his money and apparent appreciation for alcohol couldn't party all night long every night. Yes, the more she thought about it the more likely the idea of his having a girlfriend seemed. He was rich, powerful... What man in his position couldn't have any woman he wanted?

She gave her head a shake. It wasn't like his personal life was any interest of hers. So long as he kept the money coming in and stuck to the rules of their bargain she wouldn't pry. Retrieving her purse and slipping back into her jacket, she gave the room a final glance. She didn't think she'd forgotten anything. Certainly she didn't want to risk another scene like the last one by failing to follow every one of Sir's orders to the letter.

But no, everything seemed in place. The CD player was repeating the same eerie classical piece for its third time through. She wondered how much he paid the management around here to turn a deaf ear to his late-night racket. The study door stood closed and at the far side of the room a single tidy place setting and full goblet of wine waited for whoever would be the next person to enter this room. Teagan had the unsettling feeling the next human visitor would be her and then thrust aside the thought. What scenario was her imagination concocting now? Ghosts?

Sir's voice came back to her, reminding her of how he had called her over-imaginative and immature. The peeved mood that put her in helped her forget any notions of inhuman visitors and bizarre rituals. Stepping into the elevator, she hit the button and was carried down to the first floor. She would have to get straight to bed when she got home if she was to return here early the next morning.

Chapter 11

THAT NIGHT WAS A LONG and restless one. Head cradled atop a soft pillow and body curled up in a real bed for the first time in a long time, she ought to have slept like the dead. Instead she tossed and turned, unaccustomed for so long to the feel of a squishy mattress beneath her and a warm blanket drawn up to her chin. This new life was going to take some getting used to. At some point after midnight she finally dropped off for a few hours only to be tortured by wild nightmares about fanged beasts chasing her through the shadows and invisible guests sitting at lonely tables draining goblets of red wine. More disturbing than any of the rest was the sense of Sir, hovering as a vague presence in the background. She felt his accusing eyes following her every movement, and she knew in his hands he held something…a letter with her signature at the bottom.

On waking from that nightmare, she didn't try to fall back asleep. It seemed best to stay up and fill her mind with ordinary everyday things until the after-effects of the bad dreams faded away. At times like this, she thought, sitting up in bed and staring at a stained bit of wallpaper on the far wall, it would be nice to have a TV. That at least might help her mind escape this weird rut in which it couldn't seem to think about anything not involving the mysterious Sir, even in her sleep.

Unfortunately she had no television and didn't even own so much as a book or a magazine. Maybe tomorrow she'd go out early and get a paper from one of those machines outside the nearest coffee shop. She couldn't afford their coffee but a paper she could splurge on. Yawning, she propped her pillow behind her back and let her eyes trace the maze of faded, scrolling designs flowing down the old wallpaper.

Of their own accord, her thoughts worked their way back to Sir. She played with a new theory that had struck her sometime yesterday evening as she completed his list of chores. It was just a suspicion and she wasn't sure how much sense it made, but it was an idea she couldn't quite get out of her head. Suppose Sir's weird ritual was all just an act—a pretense to hide something much bigger? What if all those weird tasks he had set her were just decoys, invented to distract her from whatever his real purpose was? She tried to work out what motivation he could have for coming up with a lot of weird, useless nonsense for her to carry out.

Then discarding her original idea, she thought, maybe the ritual was important. Maybe parts of it did have a purpose. Could it be one part—just one—of his eerie ritual had some secret significance? And if it did, and if he didn't want her to invest too much energy into guessing at what it was, wouldn't it have been a natural stroke of brilliance on his part to concoct an entire odd routine for her to act out. By doing so, he would be disguising the importance of the one part of the ritual that might otherwise stand out, distracting her from the area she should be concentrating on the most.

Teagan shivered, at once excited and frightened by the idea. What secret could Sir be hiding that was any stranger than the odd behavior he had already demonstrated? She ran her mind over each of the tasks she had performed that night from the list. Which one was the one—the real task for which all the others were just screens of smoke? But try as she might, she couldn't separate one particular part of the routine that seemed any more mysterious or significant than the others.

Maybe all her exhausted mind needed was a little peaceful sleep and in the morning, the answer would come to her, she thought, sinking drowsily back into her bed. If nothing else, perhaps she would stumble onto some clue to the mystery when she returned to Sir's apartment at dawn. For now, her eyes had grown heavy and she found she was, after all, able to slip down again into a light slumber.

The next morning Teagan's eyes felt achy and grainy as she locked the door to her room and left the apartment house behind. Forget buying a paper. She was too tired just now to focus on it. Besides, she was running behind. It was a gray, chilly day out and the last of the snow still blanketed the ground in muddy, melting heaps along the edges of the streets.

The sidewalks at least had been cleared and sprinkled with salt so Teagan didn't have to watch her step as she hurried off on her way to Sir's. Taxis were too expensive, and she couldn't afford to let them eat up her money taking her someplace her legs were perfectly capable of carrying her. She'd just remember to start out earlier in the future, she told herself. Sir's apartment complex wasn't anywhere near her neighborhood.

She made it past the doorman without any trouble this time. She didn't know if Sir had given him instructions to always let her pass unquestioned or if he had merely given up trying to keep her out. Then again, her new, cleaner look probably didn't hurt her cause any either. The elevator was beginning to feel like her second home as it carried her up to the penthouse. Give her a reclining chair and a pillow, she thought, and she could live here as comfortably as her new apartment. More so maybe. The elevator had lulling music and a clean smell.

Stepping out into Sir's living room she was unsurprised to find the entire place exactly as she had left it. The wine was still in its goblet, untouched. The

CD player still blared and the study door remained closed and locked. Only one thing was different, she noticed as she moved to turn off the CD player. Rounding the couches, she saw what hadn't been visible to her before. A low table near the center of the room had been knocked over and there was a small rip in the carpet near the sunken part of the living room. She couldn't say for sure about the torn carpet but she knew she hadn't left the table that way. A small figurine had fallen from the tipped table and shattered across the floor. A pile of magazines had also slid off. That was all. Not such a big deal.

And yet its implication hit Teagan hard. Someone had been here since she left. An intruder maybe? Had they taken anything? But all the priceless artwork along the walls seemed to be in place. The entertainment system wasn't stolen, and thieves surely would have been drawn to that. She checked her first panicked thought of calling the police. This was Sir's apartment. Best to let him deal with it. Besides, who was to say it hadn't been Sir himself returning during the night to make this mess? Maybe it was even his mysterious guest, showing up after all.

"Sir?" Teagan called out into the silence. "Is anyone here?" There was no answer, but then she hadn't really expected one.

Summoning her courage, she moved from room to room. No one lurked behind the shadowed doorways or beneath the furniture. Nothing else appeared to have been disturbed or taken. Returning to the living room she put the coffee table to rights and swept up the broken statue. Maybe Sir wouldn't notice it was missing, she thought hopefully. The tear in the rug, however, was another matter. Would he hold her responsible for that? The carpet looked expensive.

Never mind, she told herself. He couldn't possibly blame her for something that had happened while she wasn't here. All the same, she gave in to the temptation to drag a nearby armchair over a foot or two to cover the spot. With any luck he wouldn't notice it. Having done what she could about the problem, she next turned her attention to clearing away the dishes from the night before. It was a simple enough chore since they hadn't been touched and didn't even need washing. The heavy silence was a relief after the blaring noise of the CD player at least, as she moved on into the den. She took the brass key from its place, unlocked the study door, and replaced the key beneath the music box.

Not until she straightened from the desk did she notice a faint movement from the corner of her eye. A thick scarlet drapery hanging over the wall behind the desk rustled. For a moment Teagan was paralyzed, mentally replaying the last frightening confrontation that had taken place in this room on a morning similar to this. An instant later, however, her fears were relieved as the curtain moved again and she realized it was only a faint stirring of air coming through a hidden window that had set the curtains fluttering. She hadn't even noticed there was a window behind the desk.

She pulled the curtain back to peer behind it. She

could see why the opening had been intentionally concealed by the thick draperies. It was a big window but provided an ugly view, looking out over the fire escape and down onto an alley below. There was a tall privacy fence between the fancy apartment complex and its neighboring buildings, but from this vantage point, the alley was still clearly visible on the other side.

Teagan thought an intruder could easily bypass the doorman and elevator altogether and climb the row of garbage cans in the alley to clamber over the fence and drop down onto the apartment complex's lawn. From there they could scramble up the fire escape and enter through the window. They would have to be a good climber, though, and have little fear of heights to make such a dangerous climb. Then too, the window would have to have been left open for them. Was this, she wondered, the secret method of entry used by Sir's mystery guest?

It didn't make much sense of course. A friend of Sir's would have nothing to fear by merely entering his apartment the normal way. All the same, as she carefully drew the window closed, she resolved the next time she came to this place to carry out her tasks she would make a quick check behind these same curtains. If the window had been opened again, surely that would mean something. Wouldn't it?

Returning to the desk and scanning Sir's note, left the night before, she found only one more instruction left on the list. He had left a little blank space at the bottom of the note and ordered she write down an address in this area where she could be reached. Her payment would be delivered there. As she took up a pen out of a fancy pen-cup and scratched out the address of her new apartment, Teagan thought wryly that a week ago if he had asked for her address she would've given him the location of her cardboard box in that back alley. A lot had changed since then.

Leaving the note on the desk, she exited the den, gave a final, hasty glance around her, and departed.

Chapter 12

TEAGAN BOUGHT A NEWSPAPER AND a stack of magazines from a corner newsstand and spent the rest of the morning in her apartment flipping through them. It wasn't sheer boredom or even idle curiosity motivating her. Although she had yet to hear back from Dr. Mortimer Green, she was already proceeding as if there was an agreement between them, an agreement that supplied her with plenty of reason to find out all she could about her employer.

She did make an interesting discovery in one of the magazines. The business section had an entire spread on NationBank and how, under the guidance of Mr. J. Rotham, it was emerging as one of the top financial institutions in the country.

There was no other information about Sir in the article, not even a mention of his full name, but there was a large picture of him taking up most of the page. She tore out the article and its accompanying picture and laid them on the rickety nightstand beside her bed. She needed to collect all the information she could on Mr. J. Rotham, in both his business and his personal life. It was an uncomfortable feeling, being so dependent on someone who was such a mystery.

Next she turned to the newspaper, where all the news seemed bad. Robberies and murders filled the headlines, which she supposed wasn't surprising in a city of this size. A gas station held up in broad daylight just a few blocks from her apartment; a prominent politician accused of corruption and embezzlement; an attempted murder near the luxurious Heights apartment complex...

Teagan stopped scanning the headlines to focus on that one. The Heights? She had been at the Heights last night. The article gave the time of the attack as just a few hours before she had returned to Sir's apartment. That was downright creepy, she thought, reading on. Suppose it had been her set upon in some lonely alley? She shivered. Maybe from now on she would take a cab to Sir's. The streets were dangerous these days. Or maybe it was only the hail of bad news from the papers that made them seem so. Yes, that must be it. She set aside the newspaper and decided she wouldn't buy them anymore.

The rumbling of her stomach reminded her that whatever bad things were happening out there in the world, it was still breakfast time. She ate a bowl of cereal, drank a glass of orange juice, which made an odd mix, and lay down for a quick nap. She had slept so little last night and awoken so early this morning to go to back to Sir's, that she felt weak and sluggish.

Snuggling up into a tight little ball atop her creaky mattress, she drifted off into a deep, pleasant sleep.

It was a firm pounding on the door that finally stirred her. A glance at her digital alarm clock revealed she had slept away the morning and most of the afternoon. She had been more exhausted than she'd realized.

"Coming, coming," she called at the insistent pounding. She sat up and glanced at her reflection in the mirror. Her hair was a tousled mess, her face red and pillow-lined. Never mind, she told herself. It was probably a neighbor come to borrow...whatever neighbors borrowed. She wouldn't know. She'd never had a neighbor before, or for that matter, ever owned anything one might expect her to loan out.

She stumbled drowsily to the door and put her eye up to the peephole. "Sir!" she couldn't help exclaiming loudly at the sight of the tall figure standing outside her door.

"That's right," he called through the door. "Open up."

Teagan hesitated. She hadn't imagined he would be the one coming to deliver her money. He'd said he would send it over, not bring it over. In fact, didn't this face-to-face meeting kind of violate the rules they had agreed to work under? She wasn't sure she was entirely comfortable with this man and his intense aura entering the peace of her new sanctuary. Still... she wanted the money. And she comforted herself with the thought of her landlord's presence just a few doors down. Although he was elderly and hard of hearing, if his TV wasn't turned up too loud and if he had his hearing aid in, he might notice a dangerous commotion coming from her apartment.

Sir was still standing outside. She could imagine his impatience. Making up her mind, she slid the deadbolt and cracked the door.

"Did you bring my money?" she asked, poking her face around the door.

"Let me in," he answered in a strange tone. "We need to talk." There was a different look about him today than usual. His face looked tense and weary, and he seemed to be having trouble standing still. His foot tapped impatiently on the carpeted floor.

Teagan frowned, trying to hide her nervousness. Did he somehow guess at her plan involving Dr. Green? Was that what brought him here? She stalled for time, looking for excuses to keep him out in the hall. "I'm sorry, but I don't think—"

He didn't wait for her to finish but shoved the door open and pushed his way in. "I'm not very concerned with what you think at the moment," he said, sounding a little like his usual arrogant self. "I need to know what you did last night in my apartment."

Teagan grimaced. So he had noticed the torn rug and the broken statue. "I didn't do anything, I swear," she hastened to explain. "The damage was done between the time I left in the evening and returned this morning."

"What are you babbling about?" he asked. "I'm referring to the tasks I set for you. Did you complete all of them?"

So he wasn't upset about the mess. Teagan was relieved and yet confused. If he hadn't noticed the change in his apartment what was it that brought him here in such an urgent state?

"I did everything you asked me to," she answered. "I followed your instructions perfectly."

"You're sure of that?" he asked. "You couldn't have forgotten anything?"

What put that odd light in his eyes, Teagan wondered. Was this some kind of trap? Another one of his tests? Well if it was, she was fairly confident she could pass it. "I'm positive I did everything," she said firmly, looking him in the eye. A sudden thought came to mind. "Maybe," she said casually, "you could tell me specifically what it is you're so concerned about my having carried out properly."

He didn't take the bait. "Repeat back to me all of your actions both times you visited my apartment during the last twenty-four hours."

Teagan sighed. "I arrived a few minutes before seven-thirty," she began. One at a time, she ticked off for him all of the tasks she had carried out last night. "This morning," she continued, "things were slightly different. When I showed up I found there had been a tear sliced into the rug and a table had been overturned—"

"I'm aware of those things," he interrupted. "Skip that part."

So Teagan went on to describe how she had undone all of her work of the night before and had slipped out of the apartment again.

"Is that all?" he questioned slowly.

Teagan didn't understand the importance he seemed to place on her answer. He was trying to appear controlled, but she sensed a deep restlessness stirring beneath his surface. It reminded her of their more violent encounters in the past and made her anxious to see him on his way.

"Yes, that's all," she said. "Except the part you didn't want to hear about, where I cleaned up the broken statue and searched the rooms for intruders. And shut the window."

"What?" he asked. "There was an open window?" For a moment he had seemed to be relaxing, as if some inner fear had been laid to rest. Now he was alert again, and a tense note had slipped into his voice.

"Yes, there was a draft coming from behind the drapes in the den. I saw there was an open window, and I closed it. Nothing else happened."

He appeared far from reassured. In fact, something flickered in his eyes—something Teagan could almost call fear—or concern at least. She didn't want to know what could make a man like Sir afraid.

"Listen," she said uneasily. "I've told you all I can. I'm sorry, but I think you're going to have to go now. And I would really prefer you didn't come to my apartment again. It's outside our agreement, remember?"

Her words must have drawn him away from whatever problem was distracting him because he finally appeared to notice his surroundings. He looked around him with a critical eye. "You live here?" he asked. For once there was no touch of mockery in his tone. Teagan could see him taking in the rusted plumbing, the sagging bed, and the stained walls.

"Quite comfortably," she said, feeling defensive of her new home. "I find it a little more pleasant than sleeping under the sky. Now, if you don't mind…"

He didn't take the hint. Dragging up a rickety chair, he invited himself to sit, propping his shoes up on another chair. They were fine shoes and looked as out of place as could be amid their unimpressive surroundings—much like their owner. Teagan didn't know if it was the way he perused her apartment or simply his presence that suddenly made her tiny little space less homey. Either way, she was eager to be rid of him and his condescending looks.

"You know, you could do better," he said, breaking into her thoughts. "I pay well enough to afford you a safer—and cleaner—atmosphere to sleep in at night."

Teagan stiffened. "My atmosphere is perfectly pleasant and my sleep is none of your business." As if to mock her defense, a small brown mouse suddenly skittered across the floor to disappear beneath the minifridge. Teagan sniffed. "Just need one or two traps around here," she said, "and I'll have the place cleared out in no time."

One of her neighbors, in the next apartment over, chose that very moment to let out a loud peal of laughter and to throw something hard against the thin wall dividing their apartments. Teagan winced at the noisy *thunk*, and avoided Sir's pointed look. There was nothing wrong with this place—nothing that wouldn't quickly feel righted the moment he was gone.

Aloud, she excused, "The neighbors are a bit boisterous. Happy people. They keep...happy, day and night." *So much so, I hardly get a wink of sleep.* She kept the thought to herself. "So you see," she added, "I'm surrounded by good company, an excellent, sturdy roof overhead, and my kitchen cabinets are stocked to overflowing."

He smirked. "Indeed. You live in plenty."

Teagan frowned. "What's that? Sarcasm? You know, if you think you're too good to grace my impoverished doorway—"

He held up a hand, forestalling her. "Forgive me. I see I've overstepped the bounds of courtesy."

Teagan reddened at his mockery. "Wouldn't be the first time..." she mumbled under her breath, and immediately knew she hadn't mumbled enough. Clearly, he'd caught the remark. Only, it didn't seem to irk him as she'd meant it to. Instead, his expression grew closed, distracted, and she knew his mind had slipped back to that other concern he had been temporarily distracted from. In a single moment, all his energy appeared to evaporate and he looked weary again. Well, whatever his troubles were, she wanted no part of them.

She quit beating around the bush. "It's time for you to go," she announced suddenly, bluntly.

She had expected some argument from him but he appeared too preoccupied with his thoughts even to notice her rudeness. "Yes," he said as if to himself. "I can do nothing more here. It's time I checked in at the office." He rose from his seat.

The office this late in the day? The man was truly a workaholic. Teagan kept that thought to herself however, relieved simply to see the back of him as he stepped wordlessly out the door and disappeared down the hall. It was almost as if he had forgotten she was there. He hadn't said a word about when she was to come over next, hadn't even mentioned her pay. She knew she ought to be concerned about that but somehow he had put her into such an uncomfortable mood she couldn't care. She would give it some time and if the money never arrived, she would go looking for it. She made the resolution reluctantly, for she was far from eager to return to Sir's place again anytime soon.

Chapter 13

IT WASN'T UNTIL EVENING APPROACHED that Teagan finally decided no money was coming. Either she was being cheated, or she had simply been forgotten. Whichever it was, it grew clear if she wanted the promised reward she would have to go and get it herself. And that was what she set out to do.

It was with a feeling of heavy reluctance that she entered the brass-lined double-doors of Sir's apartment building and traveled up to the top floor. She hadn't expected to set foot in his place again for quite some time—not until the next odd ritual, at any rate, and those seemed to be spaced several weeks apart. Not only that, but she was acutely aware that this time it was she who was breaking the rule against face-to-face communication. Should she have contacted him some other way? Sent a note?

Too late to turn back now. The time for note passing had ended the moment she set foot on the elevator. Now, she had no choice but to draw a deep breath and force a relaxed appearance she didn't feel as the elevator dinged and its doors drew open in front of her.

The room was dim in the long shadows of evening as Teagan stepped off the elevator. The large window across the front of the living room allowed in a faint illumination that emanated more from the flashing signs and glowing lights out on the horizon than from the light of day. Already the sun had sunk to the edge of the sky and was no longer visible behind the skyscrapers.

Sir was nowhere in sight.

"Hello?" Teagan called cautiously as she advanced into the room. "Sir?"

There was no answer. Maybe he wasn't here. Or maybe he had already gone to bed, though it was pretty early for that yet. Well, if he had, there was no way she was going to disturb him. No promised amount of money could drag her back into the red bedroom that had imprisoned her once before.

A small table lamp glowed in the center of the living area—the one light in the place. Teagan passed by the embracing lovers statue and moved into the sunken part of the room to approach the light source. Rounding the back of one of the leather couches, she stumbled onto a pathetic sight.

Sir sprawled unconscious across a long white couch, his hair tousled, his shirt open, and a scattering of paper trash littering the floor and sofa around him. Hovering over him, Teagan stooped to pick up a pair of empty beer bottles tucked into the side of the couch. Wrinkling her nose distastefully, she set the bottles on a nearby table and picked up the paper trash littering the floor. On close inspection, they appeared to be newspaper pages, crumpled and tossed aside. Apparently Sir had been taking in some news he didn't like. Bad business reviews maybe?

She made as much noise as possible cleaning up the mess and depositing the bottles and papers into the nearest wastebasket, but it was all to no avail. Sir never stirred from his prone position, passed out cold on his back. Teagan couldn't help smirking at his ridiculous position, though she would never have dared do it to his face. Apparently rich men weren't so different from the others; they just drank a better brand.

Even as she took a spiteful enjoyment in seeing the normally composed Sir laid out in such an undignified position, she couldn't help letting her eyes move over the lines of his chiseled chest and bare abdomen. He was in good shape for a guy who, presumably, spent all his days sitting at a desk in an office. Somehow that wasn't surprising. She saw him as too much of a perfectionist to let anything go beyond his control, even the shape of his body.

His face held a peaceful expression now, something she couldn't say she had ever witnessed before. Even when he wasn't having one of his intense or dangerous moments, there lurked always a wary attitude around him, as if he couldn't let down his guard even in the quieter moments of his life. If a man like Sir ever had quiet moments.

She shook her head and pulled her gaze away from his sleeping form. This wasn't getting her any closer to her money. Briefly, she wondered what his reaction would be if she helped herself to what she'd come for. He probably had some cash lying around in his bedroom or in the desk in the den. Then too, there might be something in his study... She quickly set the idea aside, uncertain as to why it made her so uneasy. He had warned her before against ever entering his study. More than that, the fact the study door had its own part in his occasional weird ritual was enough to make her steer away from it.

No, there was nothing for it, but to see what she could do about waking the man, and if he was sober enough to know her, demand her money. One thing she wasn't about to do was go home without it. For all she knew, that was his game. As if a man in his position couldn't afford to pay his debts.

Nevertheless, she hesitated. She could hardly give him a rousing shake. Not without grabbing hold of those impressive, bared shoulders—something all the money in the world couldn't make her do. Attractive they might be, but the man who came with them she wouldn't touch with a broomstick.

In the end, she settled for loudly clapping her hands together over his face. That got his attention. In a single start, he was bolt upright and staring wildly around him. At the strange glint in his eyes, Teagan took a step back. What was that emotion she saw crossing his face? Anger? Fear?

"Easy, Sir, it's only me," she said, uncertain why she felt tempted to use a soothing tone. She quashed the feeling with hard words. "You were just lost to a drunken stupor and you can get right back to it again the minute I get my money."

"Money?" He focused on her a long moment before the light dawned in his eyes and recognition set in. "Oh. You."

The tension faded from his face and his shoulders relaxed as he took her in. His voice slurred a little, but at least his gaze was fairly clear. Yawning, he rubbed at his stubbly face. Teagan had never seen him looking so unkempt.

"How did you get in?" he asked.

"The same way I always do. The doorman doesn't question me by now. I, on the other hand, do question you. I thought you were going to send the money to my apartment."

"Money?" he repeated again.

Was he genuinely confused or just trying to get out of paying up? Fortunately, his memory quickly sharpened before Teagan had to jog it with harsh words.

"Oh, right," he said, stretching. "I might have known the one thing that'd drag you through those elevator doors."

Teagan stiffened, trying to ignore the way his movements flexed the muscles of his shoulders. It was insulting how he kept dangling money before her like a worm before a fish. And yet...it always seemed to work.

At least, on this occasion, he was too out of it to waste any energy on mockery. "Hold on," he said. "I'll get my checkbook." The pronouncement was followed by a very wobbly attempt at climbing to his feet that nearly landed him on the floor.

Before she knew what she was doing, Teagan had ducked in to catch him. "Whoa! Slow down," she said. "Take it easy." As she eased him back onto the couch, she tried not to concentrate on how firm his muscled chest felt beneath her palm. The faint scent of his cologne drifted to her, mingling with the clinging beer fumes in a way that was strangely pleasant. She realized this was the first time she had ever been so close to him when there wasn't some sort of tense confrontation underway between them. It was an unexpectedly warming experience.

He shot her a calculating look as if he knew the direction of her thoughts. Was it her imagination or was he leaning on her a little longer than necessary? And was there a faint expression of humor tugging at the corner of his mouth?

Quickly, she drew away again. "Look," she said, wiping her suddenly sweaty palms on her jeans. She hoped he didn't notice the action. "Suppose you just tell me where the checkbook is and I'll bring it to you."

He smiled. "I'm not sure you're exactly the kind of girl I want to hand my checkbook over to. But then, under the circumstances, I don't have a lot of choice, do I?"

"No, you don't." She was too miffed to be awed by his good looks. "Where is it? In the study?" It was a relief to rise to her feet and put some distance between them.

"No!" His sharp tone drew her back. He quickly

modified it under her frown. "I mean, no, it's not in the study. Don't go in there. I have—"

"Yeah, yeah, important papers. I remember," she cut him off. "Where then?"

He directed her to a drawer in his desk in the den, and in no time, she was returning with the book and a ballpoint pen in hand. Only to find him already stretched out on the couch once more, sound asleep. Maybe she could stir him again?

Nudging doubtfully at him with one foot, she received no response. His face appeared worn, haggard beneath the yellow glow of the lamp. He looked as if he could use the sleep. She wondered how often he lay awake nights, studying newspapers and obsessing over his bank, before finally putting himself to sleep with a heavy dose of alcohol. Something unexpected stirred softly within Teagan—sympathy— and with it a faint urge to protect. Sighing, she pulled a decorative afghan from the back of the couch and carefully draped it over him. Then she sat down to wait. It was going to be a long night.

Chapter 14

TEAGAN COULDN'T IDENTIFY THE SOUND that awoke her a few hours later. As she opened her eyes and peered around at the unfamiliar surroundings, she took a moment to remember where she was. And then memory returned. Sir's apartment. Still. The discovery jolted her into immediate alertness.

She had only meant to sit down and wait while he slept it off. Eventually, he would have to awake again, and when he did, she would get that check written out and be on her way. Unfortunately, her plan had left out one factor: her own weariness. There was something hypnotic in reclining in a comfy leather armchair, watching Sir's peaceful face as he slept nearby. The dim lighting and the lateness of the hour combined with her own sleepiness to send her nodding off.

Now, however, a quick glance at the digital clock on the stereo told her she had dozed longer than she should have. It was past midnight already. She hadn't imagined spending an entire night in Sir's company— or in this lonely apartment, which still gave her the creeps.

Well, she wouldn't do it, she decided. It was past time she got out of this place. Sir could keep his check. Maybe he'd wake in the morning, feel like being nice, and send it along. Then again, maybe he wouldn't. Either way, she wouldn't spend the remainder of the night sleeping in his armchair, waiting for him to stir.

Slithering out of the thickly cushioned chair, she moved as quietly as possible, so as not to wake the man sleeping on the sofa. She looked around her. Where was that pen she had brought from the den? If she could find a scrap of paper, she could leave him a note, reminding him about the overdue payment. There was another piece of crumpled newspaper lying under the coffee table, one she had missed during her cleanup. That should do well enough.

She was on her hands and knees, poking her head beneath the low table, when she was startled by a soft noise. She stiffened, recognizing the sounds of Sir stirring on the couch. A quick peek over her shoulder revealed he was only shifting in his sleep. Still, Teagan felt acutely uncomfortable at the idea of his waking and finding her sneaking around. Would he be angry at her presence? Suspicious?

No, never mind the note. It was time to go. She started to crawl back out from beneath the table, but clumsily bashed her head on its edge. A loud *thud* resounded, and she bit her lip to keep from whimpering at the smarting pain. A rustling movement from behind warned her Sir had been disturbed by the noise. She stole a glance over her shoulder to see him tossing on the couch.

He seemed restless, but not quite wakeful. S[he] would have looked away again, had she not notice[d] beneath the faint lamplight the tense expression tha[t] had settled over his sleeping features. His breathing was rapid, as if whatever he dreamed of troubled him. His body twitched agitatedly, and soft growling noises emanated from the back of his throat. What sort of nightmare haunted him, hounding him to the point where he could neither keep still nor silent?

Teagan was moved by a momentary sympathy— who didn't know the terror of a bad dream? Approaching the couch where he slept, she stretched out a hand to give him a gentle shake. She didn't know what she expected, maybe that he would sigh and roll over, to slip into a quieter dream.

But her hesitant effort only seemed to drag whatever unpleasantness stalked his dreams closer to the surface. His head tossed restlessly, and beads of sweat began to form on his forehead and upper lip. His face was twitching now, his fingers digging into the sofa beneath him, so that his nails scored the expensive leather. Teagan didn't see how he failed to wake himself in his own excitement. Another minute and he'd be thrashing.

This had gone far enough. Consequences or not, she couldn't let him continue like this. Suppose he hurt himself somehow? What if he was having some sort of seizure and was unable to wake from it? Panicked by the thought, she grabbed his shoulders and shook him in earnest. Nothing happened.

. calling his name. "Sir, can you hear
again." She didn't care that her voice was
. "Do you want me to get you some help? Do
ed an ambulance?"

.o response. Her mind raced. Did he have a
dical condition, any prescriptions lying around
nat might help? Were there emergency numbers for
a friend or family member she could call? Why had it
never occurred to her to ask these sorts of questions
before? The answer came immediately, of course.
Because theirs was a strictly business relationship,
built on a no-questions-asked basis. She really knew
nothing about him, and until tonight, had needed to
know nothing.

Trying to keep calm, she scurried into the kitchen
where she dug hastily through the cabinets until she
found a dishtowel that she soaked in icy water. One
last ditch effort to wake him, she decided, and if that
failed, she'd start searching for a phone to call for help.

Back on the couch, Sir shuddered as the cold cloth
was pressed against his brow. Was it helping? She
couldn't be sure.

She tried talking again, in a soothing tone. "Breathe
easy, Sir, and try to come back to me. Whatever it is
that's holding onto you, just let it go and follow my
voice." Maybe he heard her, and maybe he didn't, but
she kept it up. "You're safe," she comforted. "We're
sitting here in your apartment, together, on the
couch. You drank a little, we talked, and now you're
having a nap. No big deal. You can wake up whenever
you want."

Was it her imagination, or was he growing still under the sound of her voice and the touch of the wet cloth? She kept both her tone and the cool stroking steady as she continued streaming whatever words came to mind. She had no idea what she was babbling about. She was too busy watching for signs of improvement while battling internally with the decision of whether or not to call for help to pay attention to the part of her that kept nattering meaninglessly on in the background.

It was probably only a few minutes before he started to come back to himself again. To Teagan the passage of time felt blurred, however. The wait between the end of his twitching and the first time his eyes opened seemed longer still. There was no recognition in his dark gaze as it flicked over her before moving on to roam over the rest of his surroundings. That incomprehension sent a fresh flood of concern through Teagan.

"Sir?" She gripped his hand and gave it a tight squeeze to draw his attention back to her face. Maybe now was a good time to use a familiar name. "Mr. Rotham, sir, do you know where you are? Does anything hurt? Can you understand what I'm asking you?" She knew she was barraging him with too many questions but couldn't seem to help herself.

His eyes gave up their exploration of the room and returned to her. With a rush of relief, she saw recognition set in.

"I never gave you my name." His voice sounded cracked as he made the statement, but at least he sounded like his rational self.

"No," she admitted, feeling her racing heart slowly drop to a calmer rhythm. She was surprised to see his mouth tilt slightly at one corner.

"I see you've been doing a little detective work on me."

"I hardly needed to," she answered, moving to give his sweaty brow another swipe. He still looked awfully dazed. She tried to distract him as his gaze drifted toward the ceiling. "Apparently Mr. J. Rotham is a pretty important figure in this town. I can't pick up a paper without seeing your picture. 'Mr. J. Rotham closes the deal. Mr. J. Rotham meets with board of directors. Mr. J. Rotham cleans his toenails with a solid gold pick'—I made that last part up myself."

He closed his eyelids. "Very clever of you."

Was he sinking away again? She gave his hand another squeeze. "Hey, don't leave me alone here. You slip off into oblivion again and there's no telling what I'll do with your wallet or your priceless artwork while you're out."

He didn't look concerned. "Don't worry about me," he mumbled, eyelids still closed. "I'm not dying on you. Just need a minute to come out of it. These dreams affect me too much..." Even as his voice trailed off, his fingers curled around her hand, as if attempting to hold onto that one connection to reality. It was the first time Teagan could recall having felt his touch without fear. She wasn't sure how she felt about that. He recaptured her attention when he whispered, "Keep thinking I'm gaining control, but then I lose it again."

Control of what? Consciousness? She didn't ask.

"You'll be fine," she reassured. But inwardly she wondered. His earlier reference to dreams wasn't lost on her. What sort of nightmares gripped him that he couldn't clear them from his mind, even during his waking hours? Thinking of her traitorous offer to his enemy, Dr. Green, she felt a twinge of guilt that was as unwanted as it was unexpected.

Chapter 15

TEAGAN'S BREATH CAME OUT IN little white puffs as she exhaled the crisp morning air. Dawn was just graying the sky but the streetlights were still the main source of light over the snow-edged sidewalk beneath her feet. Shivering against a strong north gale, she shoved her fists deeper into her pockets and wished she'd worn something heavier than her thin jacket.

Behind her, Sir's apartment complex had long ago disappeared as she covered the distance toward her own, more dilapidated side of town. Already the streets were growing crowded, and even at this hushed hour, pedestrians scattered the sidewalks, rushing past in their thick winter coats, their heads all but hidden behind scarves, muffs, and hats.

Teagan scarcely spared a thought for the passing streams of strangers. Her right arm, inside her pocket, was still tightly gripping the check from Sir, that little scrap of paper that had caused so much difficulty yesterday. Mentally, she kept replaying the night before, trying to remember at what point she had nodded off during the hours before dawn, her head resting on the arm of the sofa and her hand still curled around Sir's.

When she awoke, hours later, Sir's hand had been replaced by a stiff piece of paper with a lot of zeros on it, tucked into her palm. Which of them had dropped off first during the night, she still wasn't sure, but there was no question who was the first to stir. Sir was already long gone from the place by the time she woke and hadn't left so much as a note behind. Aside from her grogginess and the check in her pocket, there was nothing to prove to her last night hadn't all been a dream.

She wondered if he always arose so early, or if he was merely eager to be away before she could bombard him with questions about what had happened. And she wanted to do exactly that. She remembered his shuddering body, his grinding jaw and clenched fists. Had it been nothing more than a random nightmare that had reduced him to such a state? She couldn't believe it. Something was very wrong there, and she couldn't shake the suspicion it all tied in with Sir's weird late night rituals.

She was so focused on her thoughts she almost didn't notice the first time it happened. Someone, a stranger out of the crowd, jostled her elbow in passing, before striding quickly on without a word. You got used to being bumped and pushed on the sidewalks of a city this size. Teagan thought nothing of it, until a few minutes later when she was again brushed by a man coming from the opposite direction. Was she wrong in thinking it was the same man? Probably. A lot of people in the city owned blue coats.

Still, the coincidence was enough to pull her out of her reverie. People had their purses snatched and their pockets picked on these streets every day. She couldn't afford to let her attention stray like this. She snapped her thoughts back from the puzzle of Sir and focused on her surroundings. An intersection was coming up and she paused, along with a line of other pedestrians, to wait for a *WALK* signal.

On the street behind her, a horn suddenly blared and the squeal of tires, followed by a crash, announced the occurrence of another fender bender in a city that saw its share of accidents every day. Teagan was among those who turned to glance curiously over their shoulders at the commotion. If she hadn't done that, she might not have seen him, the blue-coated stranger, following behind her.

She didn't know why she immediately thought of that word: following. There was nothing to say he didn't have a legitimate reason for turning around and heading back this direction again. And even if he didn't, she was surrounded by a crowd of other pedestrians. He could be trailing any one of them, as easily as her. But he wasn't. She knew that the moment she laid eyes on him this time. It was her he had jostled twice, her he was circling, and her his eyes were fixed on during the split second she glanced back at him.

For a brief moment, their gazes met. Teagan drew a sharp breath. There was something unsettling, something threatening in his posture, even as his face was too far away to be read. All she could be sure of was she had never seen this man before. And he was watching her. Equally obvious, he didn't want to be discovered watching her. She had no sooner turned and caught his eye, than he whirled abruptly, presenting his back to her, and began walking hastily in the other direction.

A chill crept down Teagan's spine and she hesitated. Should she follow him? Demand to know why he was watching her and what he wanted? The idea didn't seem like a safe one. Briefly, she remembered the violent newspaper headlines only yesterday about robberies and attacks in dark alleys. There was no question there was evil in this city. Did she really want to confront it face-to-face?

At that very moment, the *WALK* sign lit up and around her people began moving forward in a steady stream that carried her with it. Teagan caught a final glimpse of a retreating blue clad back through the crowd, and then her mysterious follower was gone, lost among the sea of unfamiliar faces. Shaking her head, Teagan allowed herself to be propelled onward by the momentum of the crowd. Was she letting her imagination carry her away? Sir had accused her of having an overly active imagination. Most likely the stranger was just looking for an easy mark, an unsuspecting passerby with an accessible pocket. She tried to put the incident from her mind as she walked on.

The post office was right around the corner. She

was about to pass it by when it occurred to her she might step in and check her box. It seemed very early to expect any response to her secret letter to Dr. Green, but it wouldn't hurt to be sure.

The inside of the post office was as cold as she remembered it. Did they never turn the heat up in here, she wondered. She couldn't decide if her footsteps really rang unnaturally loud on the tiled floor or if it were only her own nerves telling her so. Certainly none of the strangers milling around seemed to notice her.

"Easy," she whispered to herself. There was no good reason for the nervous flutter she felt in the pit of her stomach.

Despite the reassurance, her heart beat a little faster as she inserted her tiny key into one shiny box nestling in an entire wall of identical ones. There was no squeal of the hinged door, or anything so dramatic, as the box opened. But there it was. A single white envelope resting in the bottom of the box. She didn't reach in for it immediately, but stood frozen, staring at the answer she'd been waiting for.

A wave of misgiving washed over her. This was it then. No more questioning her actions in penning that hasty letter, no more debating with herself over whether or not the gains were worth the risk. The decision, whatever it may be, had been wrested from her hands.

Back in the safety and comparative warmth of her one room apartment, Teagan slipped out of her jacket and sat on the edge of the bed, dragging off her shoes. Wiggling her fingers to work some warmth back into the stiff digits, she dug around in the pocket of her discarded jacket to retrieve the letter clumsily stuffed inside for safe keeping. She hadn't wanted to read it in the post office. Somehow this traitorous pact she was entering into seemed too private to be done in such a crowded place.

Her hands trembled slightly as she tore at the envelope. Why so nervous, she asked herself, but had no answer. The fact the mysterious Dr. Green had responded to her letter at all was mildly surprising. She'd half managed to convince herself, during the days since mailing it off, she would probably never hear anything back.

It was quite possible Dr. Green was merely writing to ask that this strange, crazy woman not contact him again with her bizarre offers.

But he wasn't. That became evident as she scanned the first tidy lines marching across the paper.

A few minutes later, she sat shakily on the edge of the bed, staring at nothing. The letter from Dr. Green had already been carefully refolded and stuffed back into its envelope. It rested safely in the bottom drawer of the rickety stand beside her bed. She wasn't sure whom she was hiding it from. She might as well have left it openly on the table as there was no one around to see it anyway.

But its contents had left her unsettled and filled with the guilty urge to bury the note somewhere, much like a killer burying the evidence that might convict him. She tried to shake away such morbid thoughts. What was she afraid of? The answer to that came back quickly enough. Sir. What would he do to her if he ever got wind of the plot forming between her and his enemy? But he couldn't know, could he?

Besides, her more practical side chipped in, she was letting her overactive imagination weave too dark a picture here. It wasn't as if there was anything that devious going on. Dr. Green had asked her to spy on Sir's movements, to record any "unusual" actions in brief notes to be ailed to him daily.

Where was the harm in that? She couldn't imagine what such updates could possibly do, either in favor of Dr. Green or to harm Sir. Certainly she didn't see how the doctor got any sort of vengeance out of it. But if so small a thing made the strange man happy, more if he was willing to pay well, almost as well as Sir, for the service, why shouldn't she comply? Of course, the wad of crisp hundred dollar bills she'd found tucked inside the envelope hadn't hurt much either.

It was extra insurance, that was all, against Sir firing her on a sudden whim or any one of a number of other things that might happen. She could well have need of the extra income, however temporary it might be, and the small act of spying on her employer to receive it seemed easy enough. The only real difficulty would be in preventing Sir from realizing what she was up to.

All of this went on in her mind as she made a valiant effort at steadying her nerves and laying her fears to rest. She was only half successful however. Despite all her brave reassurances, one pesky image kept replaying itself in the back of her mind. Sir, kneeling before the dresser in his red bedroom, his sharp eyes riveted on the white envelope sticking out of the edge of the drawer.

She shivered. She was making too much of this. She needed to act before she could change her mind. She dug around in the drawer of her nightstand until she found a pad of paper and pen. With ruthless haste, born of the desire to have this thing done with, she scribbled out a brief report to the doctor, outlining everything that had happened between her and Sir since they had met. Immediately upon finishing the report, she stuffed it into an envelope that she placed inside her jacket pocket. The next time she went out she would mail it.

While her hand was in the pocket of her jacket, she made a discovery. The check from Sir. Somehow she had all but forgotten it. She smiled. This should cheer her a little.

She crouched before her nightstand and spread the scrap of paper out over the even surface, smoothing it flat where the paper curled along the edges.

Sir's name stared up at her, first in a tidy, undecorated script along the top of the check, and then in the larger, more imposing scrawl of his signature along the bottom. She didn't know why she kept studying this bit of paper as if it might tell her something about the enigmatic personality who had owned it. She noted the amount had been made out to a much larger sum than they had initially agreed on. Payment for her help last night? Or a little reminder to keep her mouth shut. She dismissed the thought. Why should he care if she told people he had nightmares?

Something new caught her eye—something she had failed to notice before. Her own name on the top line was filled out in its entirety. Teagan Grant. It had been so long since she had gone by any other name than simply Teagan it was almost startling to see her last name glaring up off the paper. It stirred memories she didn't care to unearth.

Shoving those thoughts to the back of her mind, Teagan focused on the aspect of this that disturbed her the most, and she found herself echoing Sir's sentiments of last night: *I never gave you my name.*

Chapter 16

TEAGAN DIDN'T SPEND MUCH MORE time examining Sir's check. Now she finally had it in her possession the thing she most wanted to do at the moment was to cash it. It wasn't that she didn't think he was good for the money or anything, but... Well, with Sir you never knew. Would it have killed him to pay her in cash?

She resisted the urge to dash out to the nearest bank right away however. After the late hours she had kept last night, she needed a long nap to clear her head. But even more than that, she wanted a hot shower to thaw out her frozen fingers and toes. She double-checked the latch on the door to her apartment before slipping out of her clothes and into the shower. She hadn't forgotten that weird incident on the street earlier. It was an unnerving notion, the thought of someone secretly spying on her, following her...

She shook away such thoughts as she stepped beneath the spray of hot water. She was making too much of it. Whoever her mysterious watcher was, it was very unlikely she would ever see him again. Closing her eyes, she breathed in the steamy air and felt warmth begin to trickle through her again.

Her mind strayed to the subject of Sir. Where was he right now? Was he all right after the scary incident last night? Unbidden, the memory of his hand clutching hers stirred to the surface. She knew it had been an unconscious reaction on his part, a need to cling to whoever or whatever was closest at the time. Why then did the thought of it send a surge of warmth spreading through her?

It was shortly after noon when Teagan locked the door of her apartment and set off for the quick walk to the post office. All the way there she kept second-guessing herself. She knew with sinking certainty that once this report on Sir was mailed off the future would be set. There was no turning back after this. She suspected Dr. Green wouldn't take kindly to it if she tried to renege on their deal at some later date. For that matter, if Sir should somehow find out…

She shook away the gloomy thoughts as she stepped into the post office. A few minutes later, when she passed back out those doors, she felt considerably lighter, as if a weight had been lifted from her. The letter was out of her hands now. For better or worse, the decision had been made. Time to move on.

She hailed a passing cab on the street. It was a bit of a luxury, but she hadn't forgotten the man who'd followed her on the street yesterday. Still not quite able to escape the shivery feeling of unseen eyes following her movements, she couldn't bring herself to cover the distance to the bank on foot. This was one day the ride would be worth its fare.

"NationBank, please," she told the driver on a whim. She couldn't say what brought on the sudden decision to go there. Well, why not, she asked herself. One bank was as good as another. Besides, a tiny part of her was curious about this business Sir was so obsessed with. What was the harm in catching a peek at the inside of the building where he spent all of his days?

When, a few minutes later, the cab let her out in front of the bank's doors, she swallowed a sudden lump in her throat. The local branch of NationBank was an imposing sight, the looming size of the building combining with its fancy architecture to make every other business lining the street seem insignificant. Teagan grew dizzy trying to count the many floors climbing upward toward the blue sky above, and she quickly gave up the attempt.

The revolving doors ahead emitted a constant stream of well dressed men and women who hurried past without giving a second glance to the hesitant young woman in their midst, standing beneath the shadow of the towering building and trying to work up the courage to enter. Teagan drew a staying breath, cast her fears to the winds, and plunged straight into the mass of strangers pouring through the doors.

After a few embarrassing, unsuccessful tries at stepping through the revolving doors were frustrated by her own clumsiness, Teagan finally found herself in the bank's lobby. This was a less impressive sight, despite the high vaulted ceilings and expensive décor. Banks, after all, were pretty much the same everywhere. This one was just larger and higher class than most.

Teagan felt distinctly out of place waiting in line to get to a teller. The men and women at her front and back had the dress and manners to belong in a place like this. She did not. Suddenly, the brown pants and sweater outfit that had felt perfectly suitable out on the street now seemed drab and dowdy. It was a relief when the line moved forward and she found herself at last at the opposite end of the counter from an employee.

"Hi. I'd just like to cash this," she said, slipping Sir's check across the cool granite counter.

"No problem," the distracted teller, a middle-aged brunette, replied. "I just need to see a picture ID."

"ID?" Teagan frowned.

"Absolutely. We don't cash checks without an ID," the other woman replied firmly, shooting her a doubtful glance over the top of her thick glasses.

Teagan felt her cheeks grow warm. "Oh, I, uh, didn't know that. I guess I'll have to go elsewhere—"

But the teller had caught sight of the signature on the check. "Wait, hold on," she said, as Teagan started to pull it back across the counter. "Is this a check from Mr. Rotham?" Her tone had taken on an abrupt change, going from annoyed to considerate. Appearing suddenly eager to help, she didn't wait for an answer. "Never mind. Maybe we can make an exception in this case. Just let me call upstairs and clear it with him."

Teagan started. "No, no, that's not necessary," she rushed, panicked at the thought of what her employer would say to her disturbing him at work.

But the teller wasn't listening and had already picked up the phone. After a brief moment conferring with someone on the other end—a conversation Teagan could only half make out, the bank employee settled the phone back into its cradle. "Mr. Rotham would like a word with you in his office," she said. "Take the elevator up to the eighth floor and make a right at the end of the corridor."

"But, but—" Teagan could think of no way to finish the protest. Any meeting with Sir was bound to be awkward, as all of their past encounters had proven, but it would be particularly so after last night. She had seen him in an unprecedented moment of weakness, and she suspected the calculating and controlled Sir she knew was unlikely to forgive her for that. What could he want with her now?

She wasn't aware she was drawing her check back across the counter until the bank employee brought the tip of a ballpoint pen down on it and dragged it back her way. "I'll take care of this for you," she said helpfully. "The cash will be waiting for you when you get back."

Teagan thanked her and moved toward the elevator in a daze. What did Sir have in store for her now? Maybe it wasn't about last night at all, she told herself, punching the up button on the elevator. Had he discovered some other aspect of her tasks from the night before last he was unsatisfied with? Was he calling her upstairs to fire her?

She tried to block out the awful possibility but couldn't refrain from further speculation on the ride up.

When the elevator doors opened, she found herself at the end of a long corridor. Following the directions brought her to a row of doors. Cracking the first one and peering through, she encountered a reception desk where a pretty, petite redhead was busily clicking away behind a keyboard. Teagan cleared her throat loudly to get the young woman's attention.

At the noise, the receptionist peeked up over the top of her computer. "May I help you?"

"Yes, I think I could use a pointer in the right direction. I was told to see Mr. Rotham in his office."

"You've found it," the receptionist chirped, smiling. "Can I get your name?"

Teagan gave it.

"All right," the receptionist said, "I'll tell Mr. Rotham you're here. Just take a seat." Vacating her desk, she pointed Teagan to a line of chairs along the wall before disappearing through a door at the far side of the room. The seats were stiff and slippery, the kind of chairs built more for looks than comfort. That was all right. Teagan was too nervous to have relaxed anyway.

The seat of her pants had barely met the chair before the receptionist reappeared, emerging from the door Teagan could only suppose led to Sir's office. "Javen will see you right away."

Javen? And was it Teagan's imagination or was there a faint inflection of surprise in the girl's voice? Then again, taking in the other woman's trim gray suit and dressy high heels, maybe it was no wonder she was surprised Sir would usher a woman like Teagan into his office, as if she were someone of importance. Once again, Teagan regretted her choice of clothing for this outing, but it was too late to do anything about it now.

Thanking the other woman, she summoned her courage and stepped through the door into Sir's office. There, she stopped short. Somehow she had expected a more conventional setting with a computer desk and maybe a couple of chairs packed into a closet sized room. There should be a withered potted tree in the corner and a single framed photo sitting on the edge of a cluttered desk. She should have known realized Sir would never suffer anything so drab and spartan.

His private office was as large as the living room of his home and nearly as lavish. There was a long oak meeting table surrounded by chairs at the far side of the room, along with an assortment of electronic equipment she guessed had something to do with playing slide projections and recording meetings.

To his credit, Sir seemed to be hard at work in the more business oriented end of his office at the moment. His back toward her, he leaned over a stack of folders and a scattering of loose papers with an absorbed attitude. Well, if he was extremely busy she could always come back another time, Teagan thought with relief. Almost before her brain knew what her feet were doing, she was backing out the door again.

Her progress was halted by his sharp, over the shoulder command. "Come back in here."

Teagan froze.

Chapter 17

SIR NEVER GLANCED BACK AT her. "Stop hovering in the doorway like a ghoul. Come in and shut the door."

Teagan obeyed. It never occurred to her to do anything else when faced with one of Sir's commands. He didn't look away from his work until the click of the shutting door echoed through the silent room. Then he turned and leaned against the table, surveying her.

Teagan fidgeted. She discovered a loose thread hanging from the long sleeve of her sweater, and plucking at it suddenly became an immensely absorbing business. Her shoes also felt very tight. An odd thing to notice at a time like this, but she barely had room to wiggle her toes. Maybe it was time she moved up a shoe size?

She was contemplating the merits of six and a halfs versus sevens when Sir cut into her thoughts. "I see you found your way up."

"Yes."

"They're taking care of your check downstairs?"

"Uh-huh." There seemed to be nothing more to say.

"Good. Drag up a chair and sit down. I have a piece of business to talk over with you."

"With me?" Teagan didn't try to hide her surprise. Since when had he thought it worth his while to talk over anything with her? Nevertheless, she followed his impatient motion and took a seat at the opposite side of the table. Sir remained standing. For all his sudden summoning, he didn't seem in any great hurry to present his purpose.

"You haven't said anything to the contrary, so I take it you got home all right this morning?" he asked. His tone was casual, but Teagan wondered if this was his roundabout way of broaching the incident from last night.

"I made it back fine, thanks." Since when had he cared about how she got home, or even if she got there, after leaving his place? She kept the thought to herself.

"Good. You look like you managed to get in a bit of rest too."

Teagan decided it was time she took over the conversation. "How did you sleep?" she asked pointedly.

His expression said he knew very well what she was getting at. "Quite well," he said, with a tone of finality. "At least, I will tonight." Obviously, he didn't plan to touch any closer on the subject.

"Good," she said, mimicking his authority. "Javen." She hadn't planned on adding that last, but it had sort of slipped out on its own. All the same, she couldn't help inflecting amusement into the name.

Sir apparently caught her mood for his eyebrows lifted a little. "You don't approve? Of my name?"

"I think I'll stick with Sir," she said, straight faced.

He shrugged. "Suit yourself. Most people are eager to get on a first name basis with me."

"I'm sure your pretty receptionist is."

"What's that? Jealousy? I hadn't realized you felt that way about me."

"I don't believe that. I think you imagine all women feel that way about you."

"And you think they don't?"

Before she could form a reply, the conversation was interrupted by a light rapping on the door. Sir raised his voice. "What is it, Kat?"

The pretty receptionist poked her head in the door. "I'm sorry, sir, but your one o'clock appointment has arrived."

Sir? Not Javen this time? Teagan shot him a significant look, which he ignored.

"Tell him I'll be with him in a few minutes," he was saying to the receptionist.

Kat puckered her lips in a slightly disapproving expression. She ducked silently back out the door, but not before Teagan caught the quick, calculating glance thrown her way. Clearly, Kat wondered what private business was taking up her boss's time.

"A shame," Sir said to Teagan. "I was learning so much about myself, and we were just getting started."

Teagan ignored that. "I see I'm cutting into your schedule. Maybe I'd better go."

Sir appeared distracted. "It's nothing urgent. He can wait."

Teagan wondered what his visitor in the next room had done to earn the note of distaste that had crept into Sir's voice. Then again, maybe it was her he was annoyed with. At any rate, all traces of their lighter conversation had evaporated now.

"Sit down," he said, seeming not to notice she already had. "I have a business proposition to discuss with you."

"Another one?"

He waved a careless hand. "This has nothing to do with that other deal. It's an unrelated matter."

"I see." She didn't really, but felt some answer was necessary to fill the silence.

He continued. "There's a small nuisance that needs to be taken care of. Nothing important. Well, it's important to me, I suppose, but..." He paused, as if to consider his next words. Teagan thought that was unlike the Sir she was accustomed to. When he spoke again, he surprised her by taking up a seemingly unrelated subject.

"My parents died when I was very young, Teagan. My grandfather all but raised me. Grandfather Rotham is old and his health is poor these days, but his wits are still sharp. It was he who began this bank and built it up to what it is today, practically single handedly. I owe everything to him, and he, in turn, follows all my actions, both in the business world and elsewhere, with avid interest. For these reasons, worrying him or disappointing him has always been among my greatest fears."

He cut off abruptly, and Teagan thought he had admitted more of his personal feelings than he'd meant to. Certainly, she would never have guessed he had a softer side for family. He spoke briskly now, as if to smother that image. "Both Grandfather and I will be attending a charity event tomorrow evening, a banquet to raise funds for the new hospital downtown. Grandfather's already made a sizable contribution, as well as organizing this event."

Teagan struggled for something relevant to say to a subject that appeared to have nothing to do with her. "You must be proud of him."

He brushed the compliment aside. "Of course. I always have been. He, on the other hand, has been somewhat displeased with me, of late. Certain facets of my personal life have earned his disapproval."

"Oh? I can't imagine why," Teagan said innocently, thinking of his obvious drinking problem and his late night partying. To say nothing of the stream of pretty receptionists and assistants who probably poured in and out of his life.

He didn't answer her sarcastic comment. "Neither can I. But be that as it may, I'm willing to placate the old man, and I think I know just the way to get back into his good graces. He's always badgering me to settle down and take an interest in just one woman for a while. I gather he thinks the right woman in my life can tame my evil habits, or some such romantic nonsense."

"Nonsense, indeed," Teagan commented. "All the

right women are too busy looking for the right man to waste time reforming a flawed character like you." She didn't know where she was getting the courage to slip in such comments, but Sir didn't seem offended by her words.

"My thoughts exactly," he said. "That's why I've developed a slightly devious scheme to persuade the old man I'm really and truly prepared to settle down. For the past few weeks, I've been dropping little hints to him about this new woman in my life, the most amazing, sweet, and clever creature you'd ever want to meet. She's intelligent, loving, and successful. And naturally, she worships me."

"Naturally." Teagan tried to keep a sour note out of her voice. She had suspected a mystery girlfriend all along. She wondered how Kat felt about this other woman. She tried not to dwell on what she felt about it because her own emotions regarding the news were unsettling.

Sir was continuing, apparently oblivious to her response. "I've promised Grandfather he would meet this exalted beauty tomorrow night at the event. That's what I meant to get your opinion on. My date for the night is a clever and attractive girl. I didn't exaggerate there. Unfortunately, she has no fashion sense, and I have it in mind to send one of my assistants out to pick her up a few things for tomorrow night. I can't be introducing my grandfather to some unsophisticated slouch. I'm thinking she'll need formal attire and maybe some sort of dazzling jewelry to blind Grandfather to any of her weaker points.

What do you think?"

Teagan was puzzled. "Actually, right now I'm wondering why your little redheaded assistant couldn't answer any questions for you on the subject. I don't know anything about what women wear to these things."

"Kat," Sir said, "can be very resourceful. But it's you I needed to consult about the eveningwear."

Teagan shrugged. "Um, okay."

"What size are you?"

She frowned. "That's not your business. If your date has the build of your receptionist, I'd say she needs a size five in a dress. I didn't pay much attention to Kat's feet, but they looked pretty big. Maybe a shoe size…" That was as far as she got before Sir's suggestion sank in. "Your perfect girlfriend is a fabrication, isn't she? I'm your real date." She felt stupid for catching on so slowly.

"You are if you're interested in scoring a nice fat bonus on your monthly paycheck."

Outwardly, she heaved a sigh of annoyance, but inwardly she felt a rush of relief she had no explanation for. Somehow she hadn't wanted to think of Sir being tamed by his perfect Ms. Right. Nevertheless, suspicion mingled with her relief.

"Why couldn't Kat play the part and impress your grandfather for you?"

"I thought you didn't like Kat."

"I never said I didn't like her," she pointed out.

"You inferred it when you made reference to her big feet. If I'm not mistaken, catty remarks are the usual sign of a woman's disapproval."

"I simply think you could do better," she suggested, feeling her cheeks turning pink.

"So do I. That's why I chose you."

No longer certain what they were talking about, Teagan decided it was time to take a step back and start over. "How much money are we talking? I think you know I'm not going into this for pocket change."

"Outrageous," he said calmly. "I take you out for a magical evening, wining and dining with high society, and you charge me a fee?" But then he amended his stance. "I'm well aware taking on such a greedy companion is going to cost me. I'm prepared to pay the price."

"Which makes me wonder why you agree to do it," Teagan said. "Surely any one of a number of your lady friends would jump at the chance, and not expect to be paid for it."

He looked amused. "None of my other lady friends are on speaking terms with me at present. Besides, not just any girl will live up to my glowing assessment and impress my grandfather. I had to pick someone suitable to play the part."

"And I'm suitable?"

His dark eyes glittered. "I think I can make you so, yes."

Another light rap at the door made Teagan jump. She cast off the unnamed emotion that had begun to settle over her under Sir's perusal. "It's time for me to go."

"Yes," he agreed. "Kat will show you out and

see you're taken care of downstairs. I'll pick you up tomorrow night at six. I'll send the clothes around to you before then."

Teagan barely heard him. Her head was feeling oddly light and suddenly, she was aware of a strong need to escape his presence. She needed time to consider the unexpected sensations that overcame her every time she shared an encounter with Sir. Something in their business relationship was starting to go very wrong.

Chapter 18

TEAGAN WAS PREOCCUPIED AS SHE passed through the reception area. She walked by Kat's desk without a glance and barely noticed the nervous little man in a blue coat who shoved past her in the doorway on his way into Sir's office. As she stepped into the corridor with the elevator, her thoughts were full of Sir, their new arrangement, and her own strange feelings surrounding it all. Perhaps more than anything, she admitted to herself, she was worried over how her confused feelings toward Sir might affect her secret deal with Dr. Green.

Maybe that was why it didn't sink in right away. Not until she was on her way down to the first floor was she suddenly jolted by the memory of what she had seen. The skinny man in the blue coat... She swallowed, trying to deny the idea, but it was no good. She had seen that man once before, as he trailed her along the city sidewalks. Hanging back at a distance. Watching. He had turned and disappeared the moment she had caught him. Surely that was a sign he was planning something evil.

Why had this same man been in Sir's office? The first logical thought was he had followed her there. But the next possibility was more disturbing. He was Sir's one o'clock appointment. The visitor Sir had been annoyed with and had put off seeing. Maybe Sir's annoyance had stemmed from the fact he didn't want Teagan to see his visitor. But that idea made no sense. What could Sir and the blue-coated stranger have in common—except her?

All the way down to the first floor, as her heart raced and soothing elevator music played in the background, Teagan tried to figure out the puzzle. She briefly toyed with the idea of crashing back into Sir's office and demanding to know what was going on. But try as she might, she couldn't work up the nerve to do it. What if it was all just some weird coincidence? Or what if she was mistaken and it wasn't the same man? After all, she had only seen her stalker from a distance and his face had been unclear. It was possible she had misrecognized him just now. But her gut argued with the logic of her head. It was him. Somehow she just knew.

That was as far as she had gotten in her thoughts by the time the elevator dinged and the doors opened to release her onto the first floor. Stepping out into the busy lobby, she hesitated, glancing back at the elevator. But it was useless. She knew she wasn't going to work up the nerve to confront the two men. Not on Sir's home ground anyway. The time for that would come later.

Retrieving the promised cash from the dark-haired teller she had spoken with earlier, she departed the bank, her business complete. Once out on the street, paranoia set in, so that she found herself peering up at the office windows on the upper floors. Were Sir and his blue-coated friend watching her out one of those windows? Then, as pedestrians crowded around her and the momentum of the crowd carried her on down the sidewalk, she found herself studying the faces of the passersby. Were any of them more spies sent to watch her? The thought made her so uncomfortable she stepped out to the curb and hailed a cab to take her home.

Immediately on entering the warmth and safety of her apartment, Teagan sat down to write another report to Dr. Green. The conversation in Sir's office was fresh in her memory, and she didn't want to forget the details. And yet…and yet as she drew to the end of the report, her pen slowed in its tracks across the page.

She remembered that uncomfortable feeling that had overtaken her back in the office. Since when had she started getting sentimental? And over Sir, of all people. The direction of her thoughts made her squirm, so that she set back to work on the report with more determination than ever. Whatever these ridiculous feelings were, they must be crushed as ruthlessly as she squashed the big black roaches that got into her kitchen sink every morning.

She rapidly finished the report, folded it, and stuffed it into the drawer on her nightstand. No point in sending it just yet, she told herself. She might as well add to it regularly until she had a week's worth of information to mail out to Vermont.

Sure, that's why you're putting it off, a little voice whispered snidely in her head, *it couldn't be you're giving yourself more time to think it over, more time to change your mind*.

Teagan grimaced and silenced the thought. Suddenly developing a headache of enormous proportions, she sat down, dragged off her boots, and collapsed into bed. All she needed was a little sleep. Maybe when she woke again the world would make a little more sense.

It was the middle of the night and Teagan was deep into her dreams when an insistent thumping, rattling noise jarred her awake. Crawling upright in bed, she stared, heart thundering, toward the flimsy door that was the lone entrance or exit from her apartment. What was going on out there? Surely someone with nothing to hide would call out for her to open up, rather than assaulting her door? It was dark, but she could just make out the outline of the doorway by the lines of pale light filtering around its edges from the stairwell beyond. The thumping noise at the other side of the door continued and Teagan thought, through the darkness, she could see the door's knob turning as someone attempted to shake it open.

There was no time to think. She leapt out of bed and flicked on her lights, making as much noise as possible during the process. Scanning her small apartment for a likely weapon, she grabbed up the same pair of scissors from her nightstand she had used the other day when snipping the clipping of Sir from the newspaper. The realization gave her pause, as the knocking on the door fell silent. Was it Sir standing on the other side? That seemed unlikely. Sir would be calling her name, wouldn't he?

During the long, breathless moments that eased out as she stood behind the door, straining her ears to pick up another sound and tightly gripping the cold metal scissors in her hand, nothing stirred. Not Teagan. Not the unknown person on the other side of the door. As the minutes ticked by and it began to grow clear the would-be intruder had moved on, Teagan warred with herself, trying to build up the courage to fling the door open. She never did.

The early hours of the morning found her propped in an armchair opposite the door, the pair of scissors resting nearby, and her eyes still fixed on the doorway. Her level of alertness had faded by this time, and once or twice she thought she had nodded off for a few minutes during the night. Morning, however, brought with it a new courage.

When the numbers on the clock beside her bed flipped to a six and two zeros, Teagan knew it was time. She couldn't stay holed up in this lonely room forever, and calling for her landlord would have been equally ridiculous when the only explanation she could give for her panic was that someone had tried to get into her room. It sounded like a foolish dream now. Who would take her seriously?

Thoughts like these accompanied her as she crossed the floor, only to hesitate before the door. Pressing one ear against the side, she made out no noise from beyond. Unlocking the bolt, but leaving the chain in place, she cracked the door just enough to peer out into the stairwell. Her wary watch told her nothing. The empty corridor and the stairs above it seemed to be empty. On a sudden flare of courage, she slipped the chain and threw the door wide open.

Despite the wild pounding of her heart, nothing happened. She was alone at the foot of the stairs. Nothing around her seemed to be out of place. But one thing had been added to her view. A small, white envelope lay on the floor at her feet. She picked it up.

Back inside the safety of her room, with the door once more bolted behind her, Teagan sat down and laid the envelope on the table before her. It was plain, unmarked. There was not even any indication on the front for whom it was intended. But Teagan knew. It had been left outside her door—left by someone who had tried, but failed, to get in last night.

After a long moment of studying the envelope as if it were some more frightening object than a plain bit of folded paper held together with glue, she decided it wasn't going to open itself. Why did the simple act of tearing it open set her hands to shaking like this?

Delving inside, Teagan's searching fingertips found a single scrap of paper, folded in half. Slipping the note out, she unfolded it and smoothed it across the tabletop. The short line of scrawl stood out in black ink against the pale paper, but the hand that penned it had apparently been far from steady, so that the letters crowded together, making them difficult to discern. Eventually, Teagan deciphered the brief message:

Ms. Teagan Grant,

You don't know me, but I need to meet with you on a matter of importance. I believe you are in danger.

That was all. Just two tiny sentences on a piece of paper. But they were enough to freeze Teagan's blood.

Chapter 19

AFTER THE RATTLING EXPERIENCE WITH the mysterious note, it was no wonder the next time her door was rapped on a short time later, Teagan nearly leapt out of her shoes. As it turned out, it was only the arrival of a dozen boxes of clothes, the promised attire purchased by Sir for her debut before his grandfather tonight.

Though she would have ordinarily been excited by the famous store names stamped across the tops of the packages, Teagan was still too disturbed by the happenings of the night before to summon enough enthusiasm even to open the lids of most of them.

Except for the shoe boxes. Curiosity prompted her to peek into those to find out why there were so many. It appeared her vagueness on shoe size had prompted Sir to order her the same design of heels in several sizes. She suspected he enjoyed yet another opportunity to prove expense was of no concern to him.

Well, she was in no mood to be overawed by his

generosity today, especially when all of this was being carried out for his own deceptive purposes anyway. She had more important matters on her mind this morning than helping Sir carry off his elaborate farce to gain his way back into his grandfather's good graces. As soon as the delivery man had departed, she snatched up her jacket and dragged on a pair of clunky boots. She needed some air.

Before leaving the warmth of her apartment, she paused and cast a final glance back around her room. After last night, the crowded little space suddenly seemed less safe and cozy than it once had. Her eyes drifted toward the bed against the wall where she had hidden the mysterious note under the sagging mattress. Then, biting her lip, she slammed the door shut.

Outside, she quickly discovered she hadn't chosen the best of times for her morning stroll. The sky was gray and the low flying clouds looked ominous. By the icy chill in the air, Teagan wouldn't be surprised if the city saw another coat of snow by nightfall or maybe even a barrage of sleet. She wondered what that would do to Sir's plans for this evening, and then decided it wasn't her problem. She was growing less and less certain about his scheme the longer she considered it anyway.

A quiet amble through the nearby park would give her time to put her thoughts in order. She cut across the street and passed between a pair of tall gates leading into the neighborhood dog park. It was a place she knew well, having spent her share of nights sleeping under its benches.

The walkways here were less crowded than usual, probably due to the bad weather, but there were still a handful of hardy souls bundled up tight in their winter wear to brave the cold with their canine companions. Teagan kept a cautious eye on the other passersby, but was relieved to see no sign of a blue coat anywhere among them. Maybe her strange stalker was also being kept indoors by the cold.

She let her guard down long enough to sink back into her thoughts. Had the blue-coated man been the one to leave her the message? It didn't make sense for him to stalk her one minute and warn her against danger the next. As far as Teagan was concerned, any danger to be had was most likely to come from his direction.

And yet she could think of no one else who would give her such a warning. Sir? Surely not. It wasn't his style. If he had anything to say to her, he said it to her face, not by way of a cowardly anonymous note. But the most disturbing part of it all was the vagueness of the message. In danger from what? Or whom? That question plagued her more than the mystery of the note's sender.

She was entering a lonelier part of the park now, a space briefly concealed by overhanging trees, blotting the other intersecting paths from her sight. The unsettling direction of her thoughts caused her to quicken her pace a little, eager to get back to a more peopled location. Even as she berated herself for her lively imagination, her ears picked up the distant sound of approaching footsteps from behind.

It was probably nothing. Just some innocent old lady with her dog on a leash. Yet the tread sounded heavy, brisker than that of an old woman and there wasn't the accompanying click of a dog's claws on the pavement. Teagan couldn't explain what creeping fear made her reluctant to glance back over her shoulder to identify the other person. As an experiment, she rejected her first instinct to break into a trot, and slowed her walk. Behind her, the other walker slowed as well. Speeding her steps again brought the same result.

The trees were growing thicker here on either side of the path, and the safety of the park gate was now lost entirely from view. She longed for a jogger or a kid on a pair of rollerblades to speed by. Anything. But the walkway was empty, except for her presence and that of her lone pursuer.

Despite her fear, a spark of anger also stirred within Teagan. What right did anyone have to stalk her in this way? If it was all some sort of joke, the trailing and the messages, the instigator deserved to be given a piece of her mind. And if it wasn't... If it wasn't, she could at least learn what was going on.

Indignation spurring her to boldness, Teagan came to an abrupt halt, whirling on her heel so quickly she nearly stumbled. Behind her, or rather before her now, her follower also skidded to a sudden stop. Teagan was unsurprised to note the blue coat covering the scrawny figure she remembered from yesterday in Sir's office and from the occasion before that.

Heart hammering, she nonetheless stood her ground. "Why are you following me?" she demanded wildly of the stranger.

He hesitated a short distance away, apparently undecided on whether he should proceed or turn and run away. The realization he was as nervous at confronting her as she was of being approached by him went a little way toward easing Teagan's fright. If he made a menacing move, she determined, she would cast aside her courage and run.

As it was, her demand was met with empty silence. The stranger seemed to withdraw further into the raised hood of his coat, so that his features remained shadowy and indistinct. As Teagan awaited his response, he took an uncertain step closer.

Teagan swiftly threw up a hand. "Don't come any closer. We can talk fine from here."

It occurred to her belatedly if he had a gun shoved into one of those puffy coat pockets, the precaution wouldn't do much good. Fortunately, he seemed uninterested in threatening her. If he had any weapons on him, they stayed stowed safely out of sight.

He spoke for the first time, his nasally voice ringing hollowly in the silence. "Look, I don't mean to scare you. I know this doesn't look good, but I needed to meet with you and I didn't know how else to go about it."

Teagan licked her lips. "How about by announcing your presence and saying hello. That's what most people do when they want to talk with someone."

He shifted nervously. "That would have been okay,

I guess. I might've thought of it, only I've never done anything like this before."

Teagan narrowed her eyes. "Never done anything like what?"

He turned his head to glance around them. "Could we go someplace where we can talk alone?"

She didn't have to think about that one. "Anything you want to say, you can say now. This is as alone as we get."

He looked unhappy with the response. "I tell you, I'm just trying to help. I want to save you, if I can."

"Save me from what?"

Again with that over-the-shoulder glance. What was he so afraid of? When he spoke again, his voice had dropped so low she could barely make it out over the distance. "I believe your life is in danger."

Teagan drew a breath. "Then it was you who left the note outside my door," she accused. Barely aware of what she did, she inched closer. She was near enough to see his face now, ducked back within his hood. She had a shadowy impression of pale eyebrows and round, gray eyes that were all but hidden behind thick-lensed glasses. It was difficult to put an age to his sunken face, but she thought he was in his middle years. He looked like an accountant or a postal employee. Certainly there was nothing out of the ordinary about him, nothing that said stalker. Unless she counted the awkward way he averted his gaze and the nervous way his hands twitched as they hung limply at his sides.

"I did leave a message," he admitted now. "I was desperate to talk to you and I couldn't get past your door. Don't you see? The more time slips by, the faster I run out of options."

An odd look—almost a crazed glint—had come into his eyes, unnerving Teagan so that, as he tried to approach her, she quickly widened the distance between them again.

"Please," he grated, looking at once angry and frustrated. "I've told you, my only thought is to protect you."

Teagan cast an anxious glance over her shoulder, looking for an escape route. If she broke into a run, would he follow her?

"Protect me from what?" She asked the question more to distract him than anything.

But his next words captured her full attention. "From your friend, Mr. Rotham."

Chapter 20

THERE WAS SUCH OBVIOUS HATRED in his tone as he spoke Sir's name, Teagan shivered. Trying to fight through her confusion, she said, "I—I don't know what you're talking about. Mr. Rotham is no friend of mine."

"And yet you spend nights in his apartment."

The implication of his cool words sent a chill through her. How long had he been following her? Watching her every move? How many nights had he followed her back and forth from Sir's apartment?

She heard her mouth speak the words before she was aware her mind had framed a response. "What is that to you? How do you know so much about me?"

He shook his head. "Not important. We're running out of time. The only thing you need to know is—"

At that very moment, their solitude was interrupted by a pair of women joggers appearing around the bend from beyond the trees. Their laughter and pounding footsteps cut loudly through the quiet as they approached.

Teagan wouldn't be distracted. "Is what?" she demanded.

He dropped his voice. "The man is a beast," he said lowly, his eyes meeting hers. They burned, those eyes, with an unmistakable lust for vengeance, and his face was flushed an unhealthy shade. "He's dangerous," he continued, "a monster. He has nearly taken one life already and he will attack again, unless you help me—"

A peal of laughter interrupted the conversation once more. The female joggers were only yards away now. Behind them, from around the bend, a group of cyclists appeared.

"Yes?" Teagan prodded, her voice coming out in a pitchy whisper.

Whether or not he heard was unclear, for he only shook his head and moved further apart from her as the passersby neared.

Teagan didn't care who heard. "Tell me!" she demanded frantically, drawing surprised glances from the approaching women.

The blue-coated man licked his lips, shot a frightened look toward the newcomers, and continued backing away. Meeting her eyes one last time, he mouthed a single word she could not make out, before turning his back on her.

"No! Don't go!" she called after him in frustration. Too late, she watched him break into a run, and move quickly off down the path.

In a daze, Teagan stumbled past the gates and out of the park. Out on the street, she hailed the first passing cab and fell into the backseat.

"Where to, ma'am?" the driver asked from the front seat.

Teagan barely heard him. The words of the man in the blue coat kept replaying themselves in her mind. A beast. A monster, he had called Sir. What else had he been about to say? *He has nearly taken one life already and he will attack again, unless you help me...* Help him to what? What could Teagan possibly do to control Sir? It wasn't until she asked herself the question she recognized a part of her gave some credence to the stranger's wild accusations. Hadn't she sensed something wrong, something dangerous in Sir, from their very first meeting?

"Ma'am?" the cab driver repeated. "Where do you want to go?"

"Anywhere," Teagan muttered. "Just take me away from here." She felt an urgent need to get away, as if putting mere distance between her and the stalker would somehow wash away the memory of his words.

"Excuse me?"

"Take me someplace busy," she heard herself reply to the driver, "I don't care where."

Someplace busy. As if the presence of a crowd could somehow protect her, defend her from Sir, from the blue-coated stranger, and from the desperate thoughts circling around in her head. Who could she believe? Who could she trust? If only there were someone she could talk to.

She was hardly aware of the passing scenery or of the minutes that ticked by before she was dropped off outside the entrance to a busy shopping mall. Blindly, she clambered out of the car, paid the driver, and fell into step with the stream of people filing through the double doors into the mall's first level.

Inside it was bright and loud, but at least she was protected from the bitter chill of the outdoors. Vaguely, she recalled having wandered around inside this mall in the past, just looking for a place to stay out of the weather. Such recollections were already growing distant in her mind after a short time of settled living.

She shook aside her disjointed thoughts and disentangled herself from the flow of the crowd, pausing outside the door to a hair salon. Her reflection in the mirrored glass was pale, her eyes wide and frightened.

She didn't know how long she stood there, staring through the glass, before a strange voice interrupted her jumbled thoughts. "Hi, can I help you with something?"

Teagan jumped, but it was only one of the stylists from the shop, a pixy-faced blonde in a black apron, come to poke her head around the door. Teagan realized suddenly how odd she must look, standing with her nose against the glass and nothing but her reflection and a black and white poster in front of her.

At her prolonged silence, the stylist prodded, "I see you're looking at our ad. We're having a special on cuts this month. Or maybe you'd like a perm or an updo?"

Teagan didn't know what did it. Maybe it was the friendly, yet quizzical look in the strange girl's eyes, or possibly it was just the reassuring comfort of seeing a stranger smile. All she knew was that suddenly her throat felt tight and there were tears prickling at the backs of her eyes. It had been an emotional day.

"Yes," she heard herself croak in answer to the stylist's offer. She did have a date tonight anyway, didn't she? "I'd like—um, an updo I guess." Truthfully, she didn't care what they did to her hair. What she did care about was that the inside of the salon was brightly lit and crowded and ordinary looking. Suddenly all she wanted was to sit back in a safe, reassuring atmosphere for a while and surround herself with normality. She wanted to listen to the lively buzz of the stylists chattering among themselves and the drone of soft music playing over the radio in the background, and forget the existence of all that troubled her.

And over the next hour, that was exactly what she did.

Chapter 21

IT WAS THE STRANGEST AFTERNOON Teagan had ever spent, trailing around a busy shopping mall, watching the faces of strangers rushing past, and feeling entirely separated from their world. Even the time spent at the hair salon was nothing more than a brief period of hibernation, a chance to quiet her thoughts for a while. On the move again, she drifted freely with the flow of the crowd. She had much to think on, yet her mind felt incapable of sorting anything out just now. Who could she turn to for help in figuring out what was happening in her life? She thought briefly of the mysterious Dr. Green, who might know more about Sir than anybody did. But he seemed a vague and untrustworthy resource, one that brought up as many questions as answers. And so her thoughts ran in circles.

At some point, she lifted out of her fog long enough to remember the time. She did have plans for the evening. At least, she'd had plans before the encounter in the park... Now she was uncertain even of those. Nevertheless, she abandoned the mall and headed for home.

Her apartment was cold when she got there. She didn't know if the heating was out or if it was just her imagination that made the space seem suddenly chill and dreary. As she stood in the doorway and surveyed her shabby little nest, her eyes fell on the wrinkled newspaper clipping resting atop her nightstand. The photo of Sir.

Something drew her to walk to the stand and pick up the clipping. Studying the face of the man in the picture as if she had never seen him before, she looked for a clue as to the truth of his nature. Did he look like a murderer? In person he had a certain air of danger about him, but in the photo all that came across was the image of a darkly handsome, well-dressed man with a crooked smile. He had the appearance of respectability. Then again, who was to say what a cold-blooded killer really looked like? If people could pick them out while they were walking around on the streets, they'd never get a chance to do their violence, would they?

The eyes of the man in the picture seemed to mock her uneasy thoughts. "Who are you?" she whispered, as if the black and white illustration were capable of speaking up to defend itself. Calculating businessman, partying playboy, murdering monster... She had too many labels for this man and had yet to figure out which one suited best. Worse, above all these other images, one in particular rose up to take precedence— that of the sleepless man on the couch, clutching at her hand, as if seeking rescue from his nightmares.

Maybe it was that memory, or maybe it was a decision she would have reached anyway. She didn't know. One thing was certain. All of a sudden, she knew what she was going to do. She was going to find out the truth. She was going to unmask Sir and all his secrets with him. The strange rituals, the frightening accusations... All must be revealed. She couldn't put a name to the emotion that prompted her decision. She only knew there was a burning need inside her, a desperation to know who he really was. And not for the sake of the blue-coated stranger in the park, nor for anyone else, but for her own satisfaction.

Nearby, on the bedside table, the numbers of her digital clock flipped to a five and two zeros. She was running out of time. She remembered she had never even opened the packages Sir had sent. She could only hope everything fit because if not, it was too late to do anything about it.

Dropping to sit cross-legged before the cracked mirror hanging over the back of her door, she delved into one of the purchases she had made shortly after moving into her apartment. She'd scarcely thought she would actually use the makeup kit she'd bought when she purchased her new clothes. Tonight, however, was one occasion where she would want to tone down her pink, wind-roughened complexion to something softer.

She applied the liquid foundation so liberally, she looked, she thought wryly, as if she had slipped on a porcelain mask over her real face. The results weren't unpleasant though, and once she had added a soft shade of blush to her cheeks and a hint of gray eye shadow beneath her brows, she began to take on a more natural appearance. By the time she finished, she looked like she had been applying her own makeup all her life, rather than as if she had just experimented with it for the first time.

Dragging off her clothes, she sat atop her bed and began removing the lids from the boxes. Quickly, she sorted out which of the six pairs of identical strappy sandals were a good fit, and returned the others to their boxes. Opening the largest package next, she gasped at its contents. Inside nestled a floor length, gauzy evening gown in breathtaking shades of purple and blue.

Lifting the dress as carefully as if it were made of tissue, Teagan held it up against herself and examined her reflection in the mirror. The colors of the fabric were ideal, setting off her chocolate colored hair and making her skin appear a becoming shade of milky white. The tight fitting cut was flattering, clinging to her narrow waist and hugging what curves she had, until she could almost believe she possessed an attractive figure. The slimness of the skirt lent her an illusion of height, flaring slightly below the knees and trailing in the back to brush the floor.

Teagan felt almost wrong, shedding her normally grubby image and stepping cautiously into this elegant creation. She laced it up with care and was half afraid to sit down once wrapped in the dress for fear of wrinkling the fabric. She next slipped on the silver heels that added a touch of color to her costume before tearing into the final packages. One contained a luxurious coat of black faux fur, and another a small black clutch with silver lining.

If Teagan thought these gifts were beyond extravagant, she was shocked to open the final and smallest box to discover a sparkling necklace with matching wristband and earrings. Plucking up one of the earrings and turning it over in her palm, she tried to determine if the inset sparklers were real diamonds. Surely not. Sir knew better than to trust her with anything like that, she thought ironically, recalling the time she'd stolen the food from his kitchen.

All the same, even as fakes, they were probably worth more than anything she owned. There were even matching combs for her hair resting in the bottom of the box. Sir had truly thought of everything. He must be even more eager to impress his grandfather than he had let on.

She donned the earrings first, and then clasped the dazzling necklace around her throat. Its teardrop shaped pendant felt cold and unexpectedly heavy nestled in the hollow of her throat. Lastly, she arranged the silvery gem studded combs into her upswept hair, positioning them where they would show to advantage.

She spun twice before the mirror, noting how her silver heels flashed beneath the swirl of her gauzy skirt and the way loose tendrils of curls from her up-pinned hair drifted around her face and neck as she moved. She dipped into her makeup kit one last time to apply a thin layer of lip gloss, and then her work was done.

A nervous glance at the clock told her she had made good time. Fifteen minutes left before tonight's adventure would begin. Not until she caught the sparkle of her eyes in the mirror did she admit that was how she thought of it. An adventure. Quickly she checked the thought. She was allowing herself to get too caught up in the excitement of a new dress and a pretty set of jewelry. According to Sir, tonight's date was a business arrangement. Nothing more. More than likely he would want all these gifts back after tonight was over.

Out of nowhere, another thought arose to dampen any lingering enthusiasm. The words of the blue-coated man returned to her yet again. A beast...a monster. Teagan shivered. What if those things were true? What was she getting herself into tonight?

A sharp rapping at the door startled her out of her somber thoughts. She knew that confident knock.

Chapter 22

TEAGAN TOOK A FINAL GLANCE in the mirror, drew a deep breath, and tried to set her nervousness aside as she opened the door. Sir waited in the doorway, looking more resplendent and aloof than she had ever seen him. He had donned a tuxedo, which was probably as expensive as her entire outfit, and wore his black hair slicked smoothly back from his brow. Like this, he looked even more imposing than usual. His dark eyes, at least, were the same, as they flicked over her in bold appraisal from the toes of her high-heeled shoes to the clusters of dark ringlets pinned around the crown of her head.

In his presence, the warnings of this afternoon throbbed loudly in Teagan's ears. Luckily, she had steeled herself for just this moment, and she didn't think her consternation showed. At least, she hoped it didn't. She summoned her courage.

"Well," she asked, more flippantly than she felt, "have I been made suitable for your needs?" She hadn't forgotten his arrogant comments on their last encounter.

His expression was unreadable. "You'll do," was all he said, in the same flat tone he might've used to indicate his meal had been prepared adequately or his shirts had been pressed correctly. His expectation had been met apparently, but not exceeded.

Teagan flushed with humiliation. Hadn't she spent the last hour fussing over her appearance just to please him? Or rather, to please his grandfather, since he was at the heart of this whole charade.

"Ah, a little fire in your eyes at last," he said, with a hint of humor. "I was beginning to think you were impossible to ruffle. But withholding complements usually brings out the temper, even in the shyest of flowers."

Teagan avoided his eyes. "You're mistaken," she said awkwardly. "The anger you refer to comes purely from your own imagination."

"I see. So if you aren't offended by the lack of flattery, you're hurt."

She sidestepped the question. "Isn't it time we were on our way?"

"Just as soon as you fetch your bag. And don't forget your coat either. The temperature is dropping."

Feeling a little like a chided child, Teagan followed his direction and in moments, they had left the shadowed stairwell of the apartment house behind them and were stepping out onto the street. Here she discovered he hadn't been kidding about the cooling temperatures. The dark skies had finally let loose their promised store, and all around Teagan tiny white flakes were fluttering softly to the ground. The sidewalks were cold enough that some of the fall was already beginning to stick.

Sir took her firmly by the elbow, an unexpected gesture she only just stopped from shaking off, and led her to a waiting limousine on the corner. "Grandfather sent his car," Sir offered by way of explanation as Teagan hesitated, gaping before the long black vehicle. Opening the door for her and ushering her inside, he waited until she had settled in the backseat before sliding in beside her.

Inside, Teagan took in her surroundings with unconcealed awe. A week ago she had been living on the streets, and now here she was making herself comfortable in the back of a limousine. It was a bit much to take in. Overhead the ceiling glowed with dots of multicolored lights that alternated from red to blue to green. Directly before her, just above eye level, a mini viewing screen—blank, for the moment—was suspended from the ceiling alongside a series of buttons evidently controlling the car's CD player.

Opposite her was another row of seats and across from them an elegant minibar. This was stocked with enough champagne flutes to serve a dozen passengers. Buckets on either side of the bar held bottles Teagan guessed to be champagne. At the very front of the car, the head and shoulders of the driver were just visible over the back of the seat, though a tinted window was raised between the front and the back of the car.

Sir had no sooner sunk into the leather-covered seat beside her and pulled the door shut, than the long vehicle rolled away from the curb, slowly entering the lanes of cars. As they maneuvered through the thick streams of traffic toward downtown, Teagan wanted to concentrate on the ride, to memorize every extravagant detail of her unreal surroundings, so she could replay them in her mind again when she was home alone in her bed tonight. Unfortunately, her excitement was intruded upon by an unwelcome distraction.

Although she sat in the very center of the backseat, and even though there was plenty of room to spare on either side of her, Sir, for whatever unknown reason, seemed to be taking a perverse pleasure in crowding up against her until their legs touched. Only the knowledge he would no doubt find the motion entertaining prevented Teagan from sliding further along the seat to occupy a spot near the opposite door.

She searched for some diversion to take her mind off the feel of his warm leg pressed against hers. "Are we going to stop somewhere and pick up your grandfather?" she asked, grasping at the first topic to come to mind.

If Sir sensed the purpose of her weak efforts at conversation, he let it pass. "No. He'll have been there long ahead of us by the time we arrive."

"He's a fairly generous man, giving the two of us the use of his car."

"He can afford to be." Sir leaned forward to pour himself a glass of champagne from the minibar. Teagan couldn't help noticing the bottle had already been opened on his ride here and a number of champagne flutes already sat empty along the bar.

"Drink?" he offered now, but Teagan shook her head. In Sir's presence she always felt the need to keep her wits about her.

"Anyway," he continued, taking up the thread of conversation. "The old man is hardly without his ulterior motives." He paused just long enough to down half the drink in a single gulp. "Right now, for instance, you can bet his real intention is to give the two of us a chance to be alone. A convenient opportunity. I suggest we make use of it."

Teagan started at the unexpected suggestion, prepared to make that embarrassing move to the far side of the seat. A second later, however, she relaxed again, as Sir simply sank further back into his seat and revisited his glass of champagne, apparently disinterested in pursuing his own idea.

"I can never tell when you're joking or in earnest," she complained nervously.

"I'm fully serious at the moment." He set aside his empty flute. "If we're going to pull this off, we'll need to get our plans straight. This will be our only chance to review." He didn't wait for her acceptance, before continuing. "To begin with, no more of this Sir business. Not tonight anyway. I doubt Grandfather would find it very believable for us to be in a serious relationship and yet not to be on a first name basis. So for the rest of the evening, make an effort to keep to my real name. No slipups either. Grandfather's a pretty shrewd old cookie."

"I'll do my best," Teagan said, but he seemed not to be listening. Without warning, his hand had descended to rest casually on her knee. Teagan stiffened, but his next words forestalled any protest.

"Secondly, and this is as important as the first rule, you should keep in mind that tonight we play the part of a couple. We're attracted to one another, we're in love. In fact, you might just be The One, as far as Grandfather is to know. So if you can't prevent yourself from leaping toward the ceiling every time I lay a hand on you, we might as well call this whole show off and just go home."

At his reproving tone, indignation descended over her, but he gave her no opportunity to interrupt.

"Now if we've gotten the easy parts ironed out, let's move on to the more technical details. Grandfather may ask questions—how we met, what you do for a living, that sort of thing. I've tried to keep all references to my mysterious lady love rather vague, so you aren't in much danger of tripping my story up. If in doubt, however, just keep quiet and follow my lead. I've invented a few answers that should keep everyone satisfied."

"You appear to have put a great deal of thought into this scheme."

He smiled—a rare sight. "I've thought about it for all of two days," he responded. "Before that, I never knew I was going to be required to produce the new woman in my life."

"And what if you're asked to display her again after tonight?" she voiced her curiosity. "Won't your grandfather expect to see her again on other occasions?"

"I'll think of something." He turned from staring out the window to glance in her direction. "Who knows? Maybe we'll break up. Or better yet, maybe I'll kill you off at some point."

Teagan didn't laugh. With the apprehensive state she was in this evening, his words had struck a little too close to home. Avoiding his gaze, she stared down at his hand on her thigh and felt any lingering remnants of excitement at her surroundings, her extravagant costume, or the coming events of the evening draining away.

Sir must have noticed the change in her mood. Following the direction of her eyes and evidently misreading her discomfort, he surprised her by carefully withdrawing his hand. They rode the remainder of the way in cool silence.

Chapter 23

THE BANQUET WAS UNDERWAY ON the top floor of one of the city's ritziest restaurants. Teagan had plenty of time on the ride up in the elevator to listen to Sir run through a quick final reminder of all the points she needed to watch out for. Grandfather Rotham was a little on the devious side, and if he suspected for a moment that she was merely some woman Sir had dragged in off the streets to play the part, he would try to trip her up with trick questions. It was important to keep her wits about her throughout the evening. When they stepped off the elevator, she wasn't to gawk about her as if she had never seen such richness. She also had to remember she was on very intimate terms with Sir. And although he hadn't made her background too impressive, she should at least try to sound cultured when she entered into any conversation. If she couldn't do that, she would do best to avoid talking.

Teagan tried to take in all of his instructions, but her mind was abuzz with its own concerns, and those had little to do with impressing Grandfather Rotham or anybody else. A desire had been growing in her over the past half hour to ask Sir the question that had been plaguing her all day—a question that had nothing to do with the banquet or any of their plans for the night.

What business had he had yesterday with the man in the blue coat? She knew it was a bad time to be obsessing about anything other than the events at hand but couldn't quite shake the fears that had been planted in her at the park this afternoon. Only uncertainty over the reaction her question might draw kept her silent. After all, if the connection was one he truly wished her unaware of, wouldn't it be dangerous to confess her knowledge?

The elevator came to a smooth halt and there was no more time for thinking. The opening doors before her revealed an atmosphere of soft lighting, live music, and mingling figures crowding the floor space. Overhead, heavy crystal chandeliers hung dark from the ceiling while pale wall lights provided the illumination. At the center of the room a band played a quiet tune that scarcely rose over the babble of voices and the clink of glasses and silverware.

Circular tables were spaced around the space, surrounding the deeply sunken area where the band was set up and where a vast space of wooden floor had been left open for dancing. That area was clear at the moment, as guests still hovered around their tables, chatting gaily and sipping sparkling drinks from tall flutes. Taking in the mass of tuxedos and glittering evening gowns around her, Teagan immediately felt grateful for Sir's efforts on her behalf. One or two female gusts she saw equaled her attire but none outshone it.

So intent was she on drinking in her surroundings she hardly noticed when Sir stepped behind her to slip her fur coat off her shoulders and hand it over to an attendant. He had plastered a small, artificial smile on his face the moment the doors opened onto the scene, and now he put his mouth close to her ear. "You're gawking," he chided lowly.

Teagan instantly dragged her gaze away from massive pillars along the room's edges and the floral arrangements spilling out of wall vases and dotting tabletops. She even managed not to start too obviously when Sir put his hand against the small of her back and began guiding her through the maze of visiting guests and graceful servers, ushering her toward the tables across the room.

Almost at once, they were surrounded by a cluster of guests, Sir's apparent acquaintances, who greeted him, gushing about his grandfather's generosity in putting together the fund-raising occasion, and congratulating him on its already certain success. Teagan felt distinctly uncomfortable being at the center of their attention, even if it was Sir who was garnering most of the conversation. She was aware of the curious eyes on her, no doubt speculating as to who this female companion was.

Finally the question was put into words. "And who is this charming young lady of yours?" a middle-aged woman, who Sir called Elisabeth, asked. She flashed Teagan a dazzling smile that was at once welcoming and questioning. Teagan had the notion she was being measured, possibly to see how well she looked on the arm of the most important man in the room.

Sir never missed a beat. "May I present my fiancée, Teagan. Teagan, Ms. Elisabeth Parker, my good friend since... How long has it been, Liz? Ten years or more?"

Teagan missed the response. She was too busy reeling from the newest twist to this ridiculous pretense.

"Fiancée?" she demanded the moment they had escaped the group.

"Keep your voice down," he answered, never taking his eyes from the crowd they navigated. "I didn't plan on it. The lie got away from me. Anyway, what difference does it make? Fiancée or girlfriend, you're getting paid the same."

"I suppose..." She trailed off. Why did it make a difference?

They were approaching one of the larger tables at the center of the room. Here, nearly a dozen strangers—or strangers to Teagan—sat in conversation. It was obvious as they approached who dominated this group. An older man—the word elderly hardly seemed appropriate for him—had the attention of the entire table as he leaned forward recounting some anecdote that had the other ladies and gentlemen in varying states of laughter.

Sir pulled her to a halt behind this man. "What, Grandfather? Not waiting for us?" he asked over the older man's shoulder. The other man turned and when he did, Teagan felt as if she were looking at one of those computer generated photos that showed what an individual might look like with ten years of age added to him. Or in this case, closer to forty years added.

From a distance, the silvery hair and the shrunken frame had thrown her briefly. But the moment she caught a glimpse of the aging man's face, there was no failing to notice the resemblance he shared with his grandson. His face was older, the skin loose and heavily lined. But they shared the same bone structure. And Teagan thought the moment she felt the older man's gaze sweep over her, the same dark eyes. Only where Sir's had a dangerous, brooding quality, the elder Mr. Rotham had a shrewder glint.

He said now, "You can't expect the whole party to be put on hold just because you weren't of a mind to show yourself on time, boy." Despite his rough words, the lightness of his tone suggested this was their customary banter. Teagan had the immediate sense nothing Sir did could displease his grandfather for long.

Already the old man was shifting his attention from Sir to her. "But forgive me. I'm being remiss in my duties as host." He rose from the table and following a discreet nudge from Sir, Teagan offered him her hand, which he took in both of his. They were surprisingly strong hands, large and long-fingered, reminding Teagan all too familiarly of those of his grandson.

She sensed he assessed her as carefully as she did him. "So you're the amazing young woman who has managed to steal the heart of my roguish grandson, are you?" he asked dryly. Again, there was a directness to his words that would have suited Sir well.

For a half second, Teagan fumbled for an appropriate response. "I—wouldn't use the word amazing, sir," she offered, with only a hint of hesitation.

"Ah, but you see, he does. I can't count the occasions I've listened to him gush like some lovesick puppy over your attributes."

Teagan imagined that as a slight exaggeration. She couldn't imagine Sir gushing over anything, and a lovesick puppy was the last description she should ever have applied to him. But aloud she only said, "I'm sure your grandson has overestimated my worth."

"I doubt that. Whatever his faults, Javen hasn't the sin of flattery in him. No, I suspect you've been described very aptly, Teagan."

Teagan? She blinked and asked, she hoped pleasantly, "You know my name?" She tried to smooth the accusation from the words with a polite smile.

Mr. Rotham, the elder, laughed. "Just because I'm old, my dear, doesn't mean I'm deaf. A man would have to be, not to have caught your name after hearing Javen babble on about you over these past weeks."

"Weeks?" She had been under the impression Sir had only just recently made these plans for deceiving his grandfather. How could he have been laying the groundwork for it for weeks?

At this point, Sir interrupted, looking slightly annoyed. "That's enough, Grandfather. You give me away. A man's compliments to his love are always most effective when offered from his own lips." He gently took her hand from his grandfather's and pressed it into his own.

His simple touch unexpectedly set Teagan's blood racing, even though she understood it was merely another part of his charade. She couldn't explain what caused her sudden awareness of him, she only hoped he didn't feel the sweatiness of her palm or the faint trembling of her hand.

Unaware of her silent emotions, Sir's grandfather chuckled. "Giving too much away, am I? Well, she'll forgive me, I'm sure. Nobody expects tact from a feebleminded old man." Teagan thought the speculative look he cast her, however, was anything but feebleminded, as he continued, "Come, come sit down, both of you. Javen, let us introduce Teagan to our dinner companions." Javen began to pull out a seat for her nearby, but his grandfather shook his head. "Nothing doing, boy. You've had her to yourself long enough already, and I suspect you will keep her still longer tonight. But for now, it's my turn to get to know this creature of perfection."

Teagan detected the mockery in his voice every time he referred to her by some lavish description. She hadn't caught it in their first exchange, but it was growing clearer to her the longer she was around him. Her first thought was panic. He knows, she thought. Or, he was suspicious at least. That concern was strengthened by Sir's faintly reluctant expression, as he pulled out the chair beside his grandfather and ushered her into it before taking the only other empty seat two chairs down. Clearly, he would rather have been near enough to moderate any conversation exchanged between the two, but was helpless to do so without making a scene.

As the elder Rotham turned speculative, gleaming eyes on her, she tried not to squirm in her seat.

Chapter 24

"Now," Sir's grandfather said, "let's meet your fellow guests. Mr. Miles, that's this pompous looking fellow in the cheap suit..." He indicated a short, fair-haired man of middle years, who indeed suited his description. Mr. Miles laughed off the insults and offered her a warm greeting. "Edward and Jane Donally," Mr. Rotham continued. These were a nice looking couple around their sixties, who were both attired in matching shades of black and white.

And so they went around the table until Teagan had made the acquaintance of every stranger present. She had no hope of remembering their names, but felt fairly confident she had at least got past the introductions without making any glaring mistakes. Sound cultured, Sir had instructed her, and she was doing her best. From down the table, it was hard to read whether he was satisfied with her efforts or not.

But if she had thought her awkward moment in the spotlight was over once the other diners had returned to their plates and their conversations, she was mistaken.

"Well, now that's over with," Mr. Rotham said lowly, "you and I have the opportunity for a little discussion."

Teagan swallowed. A discussion with this discerning man was the last thing she wanted. He was as bad as Sir.

Flushing, she cleared her throat. "That would be lovely," she said, her voice coming out a little higher in pitch than she had intended. She tried for a more casual note. "Sir has told me so much about you. I was beginning to wonder whether we would ever meet."

"Sir?" he questioned, raising his silver brows.

Teagan stumbled. "It's, uh—"

"A pet name," Sir's voice put in from farther down the table. Evidently, he was managing to keep an ear on the conversation from his distant seat.

"A pet name. How touching," his grandfather said, not even glancing his way. Clearly, he had picked out the weakest link in the pair and meant to focus all his energies there. "And what all has my grandson shared with you about this wicked old man? Did he tell you how hard-hearted I was when he didn't keep at his studies in school?"

"I think he did mention it," Teagan said vaguely, feeling relief that he seemed to be answering his own question. She continued, "He also mentioned that you founded NationBank and that it was you who inspire him today to build the business to its full potential."

Sir hadn't said exactly that, but the information seemed to please the old man at least. "Did he indeed?"

he questioned with a faint smile. "I had no idea I'd been such an encouragement." His expression turned shrewd again. "You have me at a disadvantage, you know. For while you know something of my past and of my family, I know very little of you, save of your charming traits of personality. My grandson has been most free with those, but has been a little remiss, I think, in speaking of other aspects of your life. Tell me, what sort of career are you in?"

Teagan hesitated. "Oh—office titles aren't important. In reality, I'm little more than a personal assistant," she said, thinking her odd favors for Sir were really the only kind of work she could lay claim to.

"Assistant?" The elder Mr. Rotham looked surprised. "My grandson had indicated you were in some sort of successful vocation." It wasn't quite a question but obviously he hoped she would explain more.

Luckily, at that very moment the band at the center of the room started up a new tune. Teagan couldn't say where her boldness came from, except that it was born of a sudden desperation to escape this questioning. She shoved back from the table so hastily she nearly tipped over the champagne glass at her elbow and leapt to her feet.

Old Mr. Rotham looked startled as she stuck her hand out. "Mr. Rotham, do you dance?"

The man's silver eyebrows climbed back down in his forehead and a wolfish gleam entered his eyes. "Not recently, but when such a charming woman requests it, how can I refuse?"

He took her proffered hand firmly as he rose from his seat, his eyes mocking the unspoken suggestion that he was so feeble he needed her aid. Teagan could have winced, both at her impulsive invitation and at her thoughtless implication. The man was seventy-something—not a hundred.

Her thoughts were racing as they joined the stream of couples filtering their way onto the dance floor. Luckily, she had little time to consider the fact she had always been clumsy on her feet. The elder Mr. Rotham didn't give her nerves the opportunity to get the better of her.

"I'm glad we've managed to escape the others for a few moments," he said as they stepped onto the floor.

If Teagan started a little at his arm reaching out to encircle her waist, he pretended not to notice. As he took her hand, she observed again, that his weren't the vein-lined, age-spotted hands she would expect on a man of his years. Somehow she wished they were just a little more feeble and grandfatherly; a tremor here and there would have gone a long way toward easing her discomfort.

"Why are you glad to be away?" she responded to his earlier comment. "You don't enjoy the company of the others?"

He gave a slight shrug. "It's nothing personal. I don't enjoy anyone's intrusion when there's an attractive young woman around to be monopolized."

Teagan decided to be direct. "Mr. Rotham, are you flirting with me?"

He gave a half-laugh that sounded disconcertingly

like that of his grandson. "Only a little. I wouldn't dare move in on my grandson's territory. An old fox is too wise to battle a young wolf. There. Does that set you more at ease?"

Oddly enough, it did. Teagan found herself feeling unexpectedly drawn to this old gentleman—not in the way she was drawn to Sir of course, but there was something about him that thawed her cold fears a little. His laughing eyes and open honesty made her feel he would make a trustworthy friend—something she was sorely in need of at the moment. If only all her pent up secrets were about anyone else beside his grandson, she might have considered him as a confidant.

"I see I've got past your guard."

She started because the words so closely echoed her thoughts. Around them, other couples danced on to the slow music. Teagan had to concentrate on remembering to move her feet.

"I don't know what you mean." She was pleased her tone came out so light.

"Oh, I think you do. I'm a great observer, you know. When anyone's trying to keep something hidden I can always sniff it out. And right now I think I know exactly what your secret is. It's written in your every nervous move."

Meeting his eyes, Teagan's heart leapt to her throat, yet she still maintained a casual tone. "Really? Do tell me about it." As if to mock her easy words, she became aware her fingers were clenching viselike around her dance partner's hand.

He didn't flinch at her grip. "You're in love with

my grandson. And if I may venture a further guess, he doesn't know about it. That would explain your anxious gestures, your clumsiness in his presence, and even your eagerness to escape the dinner table just a moment ago. You fear being found out before you're ready to share your secret."

Teagan's fear lifted for an instant, relieved he hadn't guessed at her conspiracy with Sir. Then, just as quickly, a new kind of nervousness set in. Was the old man right? Was she in love with Sir? No, of course not. It was a ridiculous suggestion. She opened her mouth to say that very thing, but was interrupted.

"You'd deny it of course if I brought it up in front of him."

"Oh, please don't do that, Mr. Rotham. You wouldn't really, would you? It would be entirely—"

"Now, now," he broke in, "Don't get excited. I didn't say I would. Then again I didn't say I wouldn't." His pale eyes glittered.

Teagan took back every kind thought she'd had about him earlier. "You are a very devious old man," she said stiffly. "Exactly what is it you're trying to do? Make trouble?"

He smiled, a lazy grin reminiscent of his grandson's. "You're too harsh on me, Teagan. Especially considering we may be family some day."

Teagan's mouth dropped open at that.

He continued quickly. "But you're right. It is a calculating world, and if we want to make our way through it we must all be a little ruthless at times. I'm glad you're not the naïve little snit I took you for at first glance."

Teagan struggled to get her bearings. This conversation seemed to have taken on a life of its own. "I—I don't know what to say."

"Of course you don't. That's why you're going to relax for a few minutes and let me do the talking. I have a proposition for you—one I don't think you could fairly find altogether unreasonable, seeing that it comes entirely from love."

"Love?" she asked blankly. At this point she'd be surprised by nothing.

He seemingly read her mind, for he offered a quiet laugh. "No, Teagan, have no fear on that account. I'm not some silly old man about to declare his passionate love for a pretty young woman he only just met thirty minutes ago. The love I refer to is one I think we share. We do care about Javen, don't we?"

"I suppose." She was cautious.

"And neither of us want to see him in any sort of danger—not if it's in our power to prevent it."

He was making some assumptions here, but there was no way she could tell him so, not if she was to keep up this charade of being Sir's girlfriend. She tried a different tactic.

"I don't know where you're going with this."

"Then let me illuminate my concerns. Something's wrong with Javen. Maybe you've noticed it too. He's not himself of late. Over the past few months he's been avoiding me, been avoiding his work too, which isn't like him. He's becoming more and more buried in himself until at last things have reached a point where he's walling his personal life off from me for a reason."

Teagan struggled to keep her expression blank. She was remembering the mysterious nighttime rituals, the key in the little silver box, place settings at the table, the locked door...

Mr. Rotham continued. "He's hiding something, something very urgent. I had my hunches at first about this big secret of his. But more recently I've come to see it goes much deeper than I thought. This isn't some light matter of developing feelings for some silly little twit who may or may not be suitable for him."

Teagan couldn't tell whether he meant that last to be insulting or not. "So?" she challenged.

His gaze was direct. "I believe Javen is in danger. And I believe together you and I are the only ones who can save him."

"Save him? I'm sure Javen is more than able to take care of himself." Despite her easy demeanor, his words had awakened concern within her. Was Sir in some sort of trouble? Up to this point, she had thought only of her own problems and the frightening circumstances they placed her in. Now, for the first time, she felt a twinge of fear for someone other than herself.

She turned to cast a glace over her shoulder toward the table they had vacated only minutes ago, but Sir was no longer seated there. Where had he gone?

Mr. Rotham the elder picked up on her nervous gesture. "Can I take it if Javen were in any sort of danger you would be willing to help?"

"Of course. I'd want to help anyone who needed it."

"Good. Then here's what you can do. Watch my

grandson at all times. Due to your situation, you have more opportunity to keep close to him than anyone."

"My situation?" she repeated.

"Of course. You are dating?"

"Oh, right, yes."

"All I ask is that you keep your eyes open, try to find out what kind of secret trouble my grandson has gotten himself into, and if you perceive him at any time to be in need of help, that you alert me at once. Simple enough, isn't it?"

"Very simple." She said it flatly. What was with the men in this family all believing they could manipulate her?

"I hoped you would agree," he said approvingly. "I felt sure your undoubted affection for Javen would compel you. Of course, even if it didn't, I was prepared to offer a cash incentive."

"Cash incentive?" She couldn't seem to stop echoing everything he said.

He didn't appear to mind. "Yes, but I'm glad it didn't need to come down to that."

Inwardly she was a little disappointed at the missed opportunity, even as she asked herself what was with the whole world suddenly wanting her to spy on Sir.

She opened her mouth to make some light remark, but then realized her partner was no longer looking at her. Following his gaze, she glanced over her shoulder and found herself face-to-face with Sir.

"You'll allow me to cut in, I'm sure, Grandfather," Sir said, laying a light hand on Teagan's shoulder. "Teagan was begging me the whole ride here for a dance."

Although appreciative of the rescue, Teagan was frustrated at losing the opportunity to come to terms with the elder Mr. Rotham. If only they'd had a few minutes more to resolve things. And she was also peeved by Sir's choice of words. "I certainly was not begging—"

He cut her off. "You're right, sweetheart. It was a very sweet, irresistible request. Come now."

As his grandfather politely stepped back and relinquished his hold, Sir took his place before her. Aware of the elder Mr. Rotham's eyes still upon her, Teagan offered him a hasty response. "I absolutely agree with you, sir. We'll discuss it again soon." That was the best she could do before Sir swept her across the floor and she lost sight of the old man.

"No need to thank me for a timely rescue," he said smoothly, as they whirled across the dance floor.

"I certainly wouldn't call that a rescue." She tried to set aside her unsettling conversation with the elder Mr. Rotham. This close to Sir she needed all her wits about her.

"You're right. We're not in the clear yet." His tone was unexpectedly light for a man whose elaborate scheme was at risk. "He'll still be watching. Let's not disappoint him."

Teagan fought the instinct to pull away as he drew her into his arms for the dance. She hadn't forgotten the warnings. A beast...a monster... Simultaneously, some treacherous corner of her mind whispered that his arm felt good, right, wrapping around her waist, that his very nearness stirred a tendril of heat warming her from the inside. It was uncomfortable being tugged in two directions by such opposite emotions.

To cover her confusion, she said, as they moved across the floor, "I should warn you, I'm the most awkward dancer in the world."

He raised a dark brow. "I've danced with worse."

It was far from a compliment, but she felt it bring the color to her cheeks all the same. What was the matter with her head tonight?

He glanced back toward his grandfather's table and sobered. "Don't keep such a polite distance," he instructed. "Remember, we're in love. On fire with passion for one another."

Was there a twist of sarcasm to his words? Teagan had no time to consider it as his arms tightened, drawing her closer against him. The knowledge of eyes all around them urged Teagan to compliance, even as warning bells were pealing inside her.

He has nearly taken one life already and he will attack again. The unbidden memory of those words was like a dash of icy water.

"Tell me about the man in the blue coat." She hadn't planned to ask the question, but it seemed to slip out on its own.

"Blue coat?" He looked confused.

"The man who has been stalking me all this time— the man I saw enter your office that day I was there."

She felt him stiffen. "He followed you?"

"Only to warn me against you, or so he claims."

His tone was cautious. "And how much did he tell

you about me?"

It didn't sound like the question of an innocent man who had merely been painted in a bad light. Teagan's heart twisted with an unexpected sense of betrayal. She had almost been ready to trust him. But not now.

"Why do you ask?" she demanded sharply. "So you can figure out how much of the truth you can get by without telling? Or maybe so you can spin some lie to protect yourself?" She heard the note of panic in her voice but no longer cared what he or anyone else thought.

"I think it would be best if we discussed this at another time and place."

She answered stubbornly, "No. I want answers now."

He ignored that last. "You've stopped dancing," he pointed out, his tone reproving.

Teagan recoiled inwardly at the coolness of his expression. How could he be so composed while she felt shattered inside—crushed that the man she was just beginning to care for was suddenly revealed to be a monster—hurt that he would refuse to give her the truth even now.

His eyes were cold, aloof, allowing her to see just how false his tender gestures of this evening had been. He was simply playing to his audience.

She swallowed a sudden tight pain that had settled in her throat, surprised at her disappointment. "Never mind. Just let me go," she mumbled. He could have his game. He could play it alone. Suddenly, all she wanted was to escape to the safety of her dark little apartment and to huddle in her cold bed with the covers over her head. Maybe there she could sort out these crushed feelings and find a way to smother them.

But Sir wasn't about to allow her that. He still retained a tight hold on her. "Stop it," he warned, keeping his voice low as she tried to pull away from him. "We're so close. Don't spoil our plans now."

"Close?" she echoed disbelievingly. "Close to what?" Tears pricked at her eyes. "Close to carrying off this farce? Close to convincing you grandfather some affection or trust exists between us when it so clearly doesn't? How does that benefit anybody but you?"

Sudden anger made the words rings out more loudly than she had intended. Around them, people were turning to stare, but she was past caring. She was finished waiting for Sir to relinquish her, an act of decency he obviously had no intention of carrying out. With a sudden motion, she stomped sharply on his foot and followed up with a ringing slap across his jaw.

She used the stunned moment of silence that followed to duck out of his arms and scurry away, across the now silent dance floor. She had captured the attention of the entire room. It was the most humiliating exit she had ever made.

Chapter 25

SHE DIDN'T BREAK FOR THE elevator doors. That would have been too far a distance to travel under the barrage of stares from the surrounding onlookers. Instead, she caught a glimpse of safety, and veered toward a set of glass double doors at one side of the room. Luckily, the doors were unlocked, allowing Teagan to shove her way through them and out onto the rooftop.

This area had been converted into a patio dining spot with a scattering of metal chairs and tables topped by umbrellas. Some sort of minor construction must have been going on because flimsy scaffolding had been erected against the wall near the doors. It might have been a scenic place to dine during a pleasant spring afternoon. On an icy winter night, however, when one's world was crashing down around them, it was a cold and depressing atmosphere.

Teagan's high heeled shoes crunched softly over the snow dusted patio, and merciless blasts of wind whipped at her, sending shivers down her body and tugging her hair out of its tidy arrangement. She wrapped her bare arms around herself and stumbled to the decorative railing along the rooftop's edge. Below, the city lights and traffic were eerily muted under the new snowfall.

A stealthy sound from behind warned Teagan of the approach of another person. Sir? She hadn't heard the patio doors open. She kept her back to the newcomer. She had no desire to see or speak to him at present. In fact, she was fairly sure she shouldn't have anything to do with him ever again. Why did that resolution send such an ache through her heart?

Her assumptions were her undoing. The quick pounding of rushing footsteps was all the warning she had, and then suddenly she felt herself being snatched up from behind and almost lifted off her feet. The thin arms wrapped around her were surprisingly strong. They also weren't Sir's arms. Realizing this, Teagan tried to let out a scream, but whoever had her in this hold clamped a hand over her mouth before any sound could escape.

Kicking and wriggling desperately, she managed to loosen his grip for an instant, but just as she was thinking she had a chance of escape, she felt cold steel pressing against the back of her neck.

"Enough," her attacker warned.

It was the familiarity of his voice as much as the knowledge of the gun in his hand that froze Teagan where she was. Her blue-coated stalker.

"I don't want to hurt you," he continued nervously, the gun against her neck shaking slightly, as if the hand that held it trembled. "I just need to deal with him, and you are my only means of doing it." He had removed the hand covering her mouth.

"I don't understand." She was surprised at how calm her voice came out. Inside she was terrified to be in the clutches of this maniac—an armed maniac now. As she continued speaking, she ceased her efforts to extricate herself and tried to keep her tone steady. It was best not to excite him. "Why are you doing this?" she asked. "I thought you wanted to help me."

"Yes—yes, that's what I want." She could imagine him licking his lips nervously. "I only want to protect you and the rest of the city. But to get this monster off the streets and spare more lives, sacrifices may have to be made. I've steeled myself for it."

Teagan didn't like the sound of that. She had to stall him, distract him somehow, until the opportunity came to make her move. "Monster?" she repeated. "You are referring to Javen Rotham?"

"Yes, the blood lusting beast himself. He nearly murdered my brother in a vicious attack in an alleyway two nights ago. But it isn't for revenge I do this. No, it's to protect the innocent. As long as a creature like that can run free, hunting the streets at night, none of us is safe."

"You keep calling him a beast," Teagan said, to soothe the rising agitation that came across in his voice. "But I see nothing but a man. A man who is a little hard, cold maybe, but still very human. Why should he want to kill your brother? Maybe you've mistaken him for someone else."

The point of the gun was no longer touching her skin. She was grateful for that; it made it easier for her to think, though it still hovered only inches away. If she could get him to move until they were standing before the glass doors, someone might glance outside and taking in the scene, come to her rescue. But she had no notion of how to accomplish that.

He had fixed on her first words. "A beast, that is right. Oh, he can disguise himself as a man—it's the way of the lycanthrope—but he can't conceal his evil heart."

"Lycanthrope?" Teagan caught at the word. It sounded vaguely familiar. "A werewolf, you mean?" She wasn't sure whether to laugh or cry at such an outlandish suggestion.

"Not a wolf, a cat. A puma rather."

Despite her frightening situation, she couldn't help giving a slight laugh. Sir as a shape shifter was the most outrageous thing she could imagine. Until… until she recalled having seen him once with a bestial gleam in his eyes, his clothes tattered, his fingertips torn and bloodied. There had been no human reasoning in him that night all those weeks ago when he had nearly assaulted her in his apartment. A heavy weight seemed to descend into the pit of her stomach.

Her mind was racing. Scarcely aware anymore of her precarious predicament, ideas were rushing unbidden through her mind. Sir's volatile temperament, the sense of danger she had felt emanating from him at their first meeting. His ordering her to lock his study door during his weird rituals suddenly took on a new meaning.

How easy would it have been for him to disappear down the elevator and then return once she went into the den, to hide himself away in the study, waiting to be imprisoned for the night and then released in the morning? The noise of the CD player blaring would have drowned out any suspicious sounds he made during the night. The place setting at the table and the full wine goblet, those things could be the smoke screen she'd been looking for.

She tried to find some sort of comfort to be taken from these memories. If Sir went to such elaborate lengths to keep his condition secret and to keep himself in at night, surely that meant he didn't want to hurt anybody, that he was disturbed by his state and sought to control it. She remembered his restless dreams at night, his heavy drinking. Was he haunted by his own fears and deeds?

She said, "If what you say of him is true, I still don't believe he would willingly harm anyone. He has had plenty of opportunities to—to devour me, and didn't." It felt odd speaking in Sir of such a way, much as she would speak of some wild, senseless animal.

"I don't say he means harm, and I don't say he doesn't. All I know is my brother lies in a hospital bed, injured and nearly ripped to shreds by the attack of a man he saw merge into an enormous black cat. I know what he described to me, and I know the fear I saw in his eyes. He would never make such a story up. He saw the panther return to an upper floor apartment in the Heights complex, climb the fire escape, and disappear through a window. I think you know whose window it was."

Unwillingly, Teagan remembered the draft from behind the curtains in Sir's den, the open window letting out onto the fire escape. "No," she whispered, wanting to deny every word he spoke, even as her own traitorous heart confirmed them. She recalled how disturbed Sir had been the next morning when he came to visit her apartment, how anxious he had been to know she had carried out all her assigned duties. Had he feared then that she had failed to lock the study door, that he had escaped during the night to do some damage?

She replayed that night in her mind. She had locked the study door, hadn't she? She remembered taking the key out from under the silver box. She was sure she had inserted it in the lock... But had she actually heard the click? She couldn't remember. It was beyond horrifying to imagine such a small slip on her part could've caused the near death of this man's brother. But the thought struck her, if it was horrifying to her, how guilt laden must Sir feel? She knew little of lycanthropes and shape shifters, but surely to be taken over by vicious animal instincts must be very hard on any decent man. Hadn't he said something during that restless night on the couch about control? About how he was learning to control it but sometimes couldn't?

Her captor had fallen silent, giving her time to think. She was grateful for that, even as she hated him for giving her such disturbing news, for holding her hostage, and now, for plotting to use her to reach Sir.

In defeated tones, she asked the questions she needed explained, delved for the answers she must hear, even if it hurt her to do so. "Why did he attack your brother?" she asked.

"I don't know," he admitted. "Why does a creature like that do anything? I suppose when the beast takes him over, he doesn't know what he does."

"And does that not stir you to some pity? The idea that just maybe he doesn't want to do violence, but doesn't know how to stop it?"

His unsympathetic tone was her answer. "Well, I know how to stop it," he said. "I know how to silence the beast permanently." The fanatical note that crept into his voice when he spoke of Sir was frightening. Teagan sensed she was dealing with a man hovering on the edge of insanity. After all she had learned, she was feeling dangerously close to that precipice herself.

A noise from behind them broke into her thoughts. The patio doors creaking open. As one, she and her captor whirled to confront the figure of Sir stepping out into the night.

Chapter 26

"**W**HAT GOES ON HERE?" SIR asked, abandoning the light filled room behind him to move out onto the patio. Behind him the double doors swung closed, shutting out the comforting security of light and laughter on the other side of the glass. Teagan saw recognition flare in his eyes, then something else, anger, sparked in their depths as he took in the scene before him.

"You?" he said lowly, sweeping a contemptuous gaze over Teagan's captor. "I thought I told you I didn't want to see you around again, or listen to any more of your lunatic jabbering." His gaze shifted to Teagan, seemingly dismissing the man with a gun who held her in his grasp. "Are you all right? Has this idiot hurt you?" Despite the calm in his tone, true concern stood out in his eyes, causing Teagan's heart to leap. So the man of ice did have feelings after all. Feelings that evidently included fear for her safety. It was a reassuring discovery.

She nodded. "I'm okay. I don't think he means to

hurt me. It's you he wants."

The man holding her had apparently had enough of being talked past. "That's right, I've come for you, you monster. Just as I told you I would." He had switched the aim of his gun, Teagan saw, from her to Sir. Her heart leapt into her throat. Her captor continued in a tone driven by madness. "I tried to talk to you that day in your office, and on other occasions before, but you didn't want to hear. You simply brushed me off. I gave you a chance to do what was decent and finish yourself off before you could harm another, but you chose to disregard my warnings. You preferred to keep your life, even in your vicious half-animal state."

Sir's voice was cold, deadly. "If I'm the vicious animal, how is it you are the one holding an innocent woman hostage? Are you too afraid to face me alone?"

Teagan's captor gave a wild laugh. Something about Sir's presence seemed to push him over the edge of reason. "What? Give you the chance to meet me alone on a full moon night, sink your teeth into me, and rip out my entrails? You'd like that, wouldn't you?"

"Very much," Sir said dryly. "Shall we set a date?"

His enemy snarled. "I've had enough of your mockery and your arrogant lack of repentance. What you've done to my brother, scarring him for life, means nothing to you. What you will do to others—have already done, for all I know—means even less. Well, I mean to finish it, once and for all."

Sir didn't have the stance or expression of a man threatened by a lunatic gunman. "Then why don't you?" he challenged, stepping closer. "Why don't you pull the trigger? Maybe because you lack the courage?"

"Stay back!" his enemy commanded agitatedly. He waved his gun for emphasis. "No, I'm not afraid to kill you. You could say I've built up an eagerness for it. But I don't want it to be like this. Not a secret killing in the shadows. I want the world to know why, to hear you confess in public."

Suddenly, he gave Teagan a rough shove, his hatred for Sir apparently making him forget any sympathies he may have possessed toward her. "Go," he ordered her, pushing her away from him. "Get inside and tell the others to come out. The whole party. Our honored Mr. Rotham has an announcement to make."

Teagan hesitated, her gaze torn between the two men on the rooftop.

"Teagan, don't move," Sir ordered deliberately, never taking his eyes off the other man. "He wants to do this before witnesses. As long as we deny him that satisfaction, he won't harm us."

"Don't be too sure," the other man cut in. "Your destruction is my ultimate goal, and I'm not that particular about how it happens."

Teagan licked her lips and looked to Sir. If he ordered her to defy a crazed gunman, she would do it. Something about the coolness of his expression and the confidence in his voice lent her the courage to do anything he asked. But he didn't. Maybe it was the seriousness of the other man's threat. Maybe it was concern for her personal safety. She didn't know. Either way, he hesitated for the briefest of instants, before giving a permissive nod. "Best go inside then, Teagan," he said. "Don't come out again. I'll handle this."

Teagan's heart plunged. When he said he'd handle it, she knew what he meant. He'd sacrifice himself to bring the gunman down. He'd allow himself to be murdered, maybe for her, or maybe because a part of him believed the madman's suggestion it would be best to end his life. The only way to make things right. Teagan couldn't allow that.

An unlikely combination of fear, anger, and yes, love, sent her mind racing desperately for a solution, for a path of escape. On the other side of the glass doors the banquet wore on, the faint sounds of filtered music and laughter making it plain their plight hadn't been noticed. Other than the three of them, the rooftop was empty; no help was to be found there. There wasn't even anything at hand that might be used as a weapon against the gunman if the opportunity arose.

And then an idea lit in her head. The construction scaffolding. She had no notion whether she could reach it before the madman turned his gun on her, had no idea if she possessed the strength to budge it anyway, but she was out of choices. For a split second, she hovered indecisively near the doorway and then, just as the gunman turned a questioning glance her way, she made her decision.

With a wild dive, she threw herself into the scaffolding, sending the flimsy structure tottering. For a long, terrible second, it seemed to wobble uncertainly, and then, as Teagan held her breath, it descended, falling with a crash over both Sir and the surprised gunman. He hadn't anticipated her action in time to get out a shot.

Now as both men scrambled to free themselves from the rubble, Teagan feared her action had been a pointless gesture. Sir was on his knees, the same as his enemy, and the gunman still had his weapon. Or did he?

As the lunatic searched frantically through the surrounding bits of wood and metal, Teagan caught sight of a small black object glinting in the moonlight among the debris. She wasn't the only one who saw it. Sir made a lunge for the weapon, arriving a moment too slowly. The other man was already snatching it up from the floor. Sir kicked viciously at his hands, sending the gun flying from his grasp and sailing out over the edge of the nearby railing to disappear into the darkness below.

Its owner, however, was unwilling to give up. Even unarmed, the psychotic gleam in his eyes and the violent intent emanating from him like heat from the flame made him a formidable opponent. He may have lacked Sir's size, but his desperate fury lent him strength. Barehanded, he launched himself against Sir, tackling him to the floor, where they grappled. Briefly Sir had his hands on the other man's throat, but the smaller man managed to throw him off.

With surprising persistence, he attacked again, lashing out with a kick to the midsection Sir easily avoided. Apparently failing to see he fought a battle he couldn't hope to win, or perhaps simply not caring, the smaller man lunged again, once more knocking them both to the floor.

Teagan had seen enough. As the men wrestled atop the snow-covered bricks, she looked around her for something with which to join the fight. A sculpted centerpiece atop one of the near tables provided the only weapon in sight, and seizing it up, she leapt forward, planning to dash it over the head of their enemy. Only she was too late.

During the split second she had looked away, Sir managed to gain the upper hand over his opponent, and to wrestle his way free of the lunatic's grip. Teagan looked up just in time to see him grab the other man by the throat and toss him with a heavy crash into the railing along the edge of the roof. The rail groaned under his flailing weight and then unexpectedly, gave way.

Chapter 27

I T ALL HAPPENED SO FAST, Teagan had no time to react. With a sharp *snap* the railing collapsed, and both it and the screaming gunman disappeared over the side of the building. Teagan scrambled to the edge to look after them, but by the time she reached the edge of the roof, they had already plunged into the darkness below. It was a long, long way down. Too far to hear the sounds of their crashing to the pavement of the street, but it was a scene Teagan could imagine all too vividly.

She hadn't felt weak all the time she'd been in action. She'd been concentrating too hard on how to save Sir and herself for the horror of the situation to fully take hold of her. Now, however, she became aware her knees were shaking, and not from the cold. Her legs felt as if they might collapse beneath her at any moment. Then Sir's comforting arm was around her, propping her up.

"It's all right," he said. "It's all over now."

For the space of a breath, Teagan allowed herself

to believe it truly was. And then the glass doors behind them crashed open and a flood of questioning, shoving party guests descended out onto the patio.

What had happened? A scream had been heard! One of the table servers had looked out through the glass just in time to see two men grappling and one of them crashing over the side of the building. The police and an ambulance were being called at this very moment. There was such a commotion of questions and exclamations as the curious guests caught sight of the broken railing that Teagan was at a loss for words. Luckily, no one was looking to her for an explanation.

Every eye was fixed on Sir, the man who had been seen wrestling with the poor stranger who'd fallen to his death. The agitated crowd of ladies and gentlemen surged forward, so that Teagan was pushed back against the wall close to the doors. Glad to be forgotten and too emotionally drained to care how Sir dealt with the barrage of questions, she sank to a seat on the cold ground.

Her head spun. How had this happened? A few minutes ago she had been inside in the light and the warmth of a grand party. People had been laughing, eating, dancing the night away. And now, so suddenly all that was forgotten. Death, violent and unexpected, had replaced normality with chaos. And Sir was at the heart of it all. Lycanthrope, the man had called Sir, and he had not denied it. But Sir, a werebeast? It seemed so impossible...and yet something inside her had to accept it. With that final answer, all the pieces of the puzzle began to fall together.

As if from a distance, she heard Sir's voice in the background. The shouts and questions fell silent as he began to speak. Everyone, save Teagan, crowded close to hear his story. At first, she tuned out his explanation, lost in her own dazed fog. And then, scattered pieces of what he was saying began to register in her mind.

A terrible mishap. A strange, confused man appearing out of the gloom, intent on ending his life by throwing himself over the side of the building. Sir had tried to stop him, had tackled him even, but in their struggling, the unfortunate man had managed to free himself and had dived into the railing and plunged to the street below. He kept using words like "accident" and "mentally unstable."

What was he talking about? This had been no accident. In disbelief, she listened to his story, and stunned by his lies, watched silently as the men and women around them moved in to offer him comforting words after his ordeal, and to praise him for the heroic thing he had at least tried to do in attempting to save the lunatic bent on self destruction.

Sir was very generous. He insisted they mustn't judge the poor man too harshly. They could have no idea what he had been through or what desperation had driven him to take his own life.

His tone was so steady, his demeanor so calm, Teagan could almost believe her mind had invented the whole terrible scene that had played out before her. Certainly, no one else was questioning Sir's explanation. Even the table server who had witnessed, through the window, the end of the struggle was ready to allow his first interpretation had been mistaken. He now understood what had seemed at first like a fight was really only the frantic efforts of one brave man trying to save another.

Teagan pressed her hands over her face. She was hardly aware anymore of the icy wind cutting through her dress or of the cold shivers rippling over her. Werewolves, violence, lies... This whole evening had been a nightmare. Surely if she waited, any minute now she would wake up and find herself safe in her bed where she belonged.

The sudden crunch of a footfall beside her, and then a soft, light weight descended to blanket her with warmth. Looking up, she found herself gazing into the face of Sir. Without meeting her eyes, he busied himself with settling his tuxedo jacket over her bared shoulders.

"Snow's falling again," he said quietly. "Be a shame to get that nice dress wet."

He was right. All around them, fat white flakes, temporarily interrupted, had again begun to drift down, driving many of the excited party back indoors. Most were jabbering about calling for their cars now that the banquet was as good as ended. A few planned on rushing down to the street to watch the scene unfolding. Even now, wailing sirens could be heard in the distance.

A sudden thought struck Teagan. Sir seemed to think of it at the same time. "He won't set them straight on what happened," he reassured. "Nobody could survive a fall like that and live to talk about it."

"No, you made sure of that, didn't you?" Her cold question came out weak and shaky.

A flash of anger lit his eyes. "And you would've had me handle him differently? Through reasoning, no doubt?" His tone was sarcastic.

"Was that so out of the question?"

"Yes. You were there. You saw him. There's no reasoning with a lunatic."

"Maybe you didn't care to try because it was in your interests to silence him. Dead men tell no tales and all that." They were cruel words, but she wasn't certain he didn't deserve them. She shuddered, remembering both the burning hatred in the dead man's eyes as he confronted Sir, and then how his expression had turned to one of horror as he'd plunged off the side of the rooftop.

Sir must have misinterpreted her shivering, for he tucked his coat more closely around her. "You don't know what you're saying," he said in a more patient tone than she could ever remember him using with her before. "You've had a difficult night, being threatened by a crazed gunman and then witnessing a violent death. And to think only yesterday I was promising you a magical evening." His easy tone only disturbed her more. How could he be so casual about all this? Then again, if the words of the blue-coated man, who now lay dead below, were true, Sir had already had ample opportunity to accustom himself to violence.

"Did you do it?" she blurted suddenly. "Did you attack that man's brother? I read about it in the paper the very next day," she went on, not waiting for his answer. She stared into the distance. "A lone man attacked in an alleyway behind the Heights complex. Of course, it didn't mean anything to me at the time."

What would she have done differently if she had known who was responsible?

Her gaze returned to Sir. "He was telling the truth, wasn't he? About everything?" She emphasized the last word. Somehow she couldn't bring herself to ask right out about the werebeast charge. It was too strange. And somehow, too personal.

Sir had stiffened at the question. "I never wanted to hurt anyone," he said by way of explanation, his voice low. "I wasn't myself when that incident in the alley happened. I've tried to control the urge, tried to keep myself locked away on the nights when they come strongest—the full moons." He gave a bitter laugh. "Those are bad. But the mornings are even worse, when I have to wake up and realize what I've done." He glanced down at his strong, long fingered hands. "That morning, I found blood on my hands, and not my own from tearing at my study walls, trying to escape my self-chosen prison. It was the blood of a stranger. And the study door was unlocked. You might have inserted the key, but you must have failed to turn it until the click."

"And some poor man paid for my mistake." Teagan felt ill.

He glanced sideways at her. "Don't blame yourself. The fault lies with me. You couldn't have known how important it was to double-check that lock. And I didn't dare place too much emphasis on the one task you did that really mattered. I couldn't have you knowing that was what I had really hired you for."

"Then all the rest was just a sham?" she asked, her vague suspicions fulfilled.

"Not quite," he said. "The loud music was useful to drown out the sounds of my shrieking and ripping at the walls. The place setting and the wine goblet, however... Those extra dramatic touches were just to distract you from the real purpose of your coming. You seemed a pretty clever little street monkey, and I knew if given enough time you'd eventually puzzle out the truth, unless I complicated things a little."

"And you couldn't have me finding out the truth?" she asked.

"Of course not. You were a stranger to me. Why should I have trusted you? Even if you could be made to believe the truth, you would have been too afraid of me to continue with the tasks I needed done every full moon night."

Teagan was silent, thinking about all she'd learned. She was vaguely aware he had scooted over to sit close against her during their low conversation, and his arm now rested across her shoulders. His presence was warm, solid. Teagan tried to sort out her emotions. Should she feel threatened by the discovery she was alone with a man who transformed into a beast every time a full moon rose into the sky?

"You aren't sure yet if you trust me." It was a statement, not a question. "You're trying to figure out whether to keep my secret, or to bolt downstairs and spill everything out to those cops clustered in the street down there."

That was exactly what she was doing. A soft throat clearing nearby, however, interrupted their conversation before she could admit to her thoughts. "Javen." Mr. Rotham, the elder, loomed over them. "I understand you and this young lady have much to discuss. But she has been through a very traumatic incident, and I don't think this is the time for you to keep her here on an icy rooftop talking. Take my car and slip off to get her back home. I'll smooth things over with the police as best I can, but you'd better bring yourself back again as quickly as possible. I imagine there will be plenty of questions waiting for you on your return."

Teagan shot Sir a look. *Does he know?* she asked with her eyes. He gave a slight, negative shake of his head.

"A good plan, Grandfather. I won't be a half hour." He turned to Teagan and helped her to her feet with surprising gentleness. "Come on then, Miss Grant. Let's get you home."

Chapter 28

I T WAS NEAR TEN O'CLOCK when Teagan left the scene of her stalker's violent death. Sir sneaked her out a back exit, where they wouldn't have to push through the scene of confusion out front. The entire block seemed alight with the red and blue glow of flashing police lights. Several ambulances were drawn up to the curb, and a crowd had collected on the sidewalk. People strained to get a glimpse of the body lying in the roped-off section of the street.

All of these details Teagan took in from a distance, for Sir never let her get close to the scene. She didn't know whether he was protecting her for her own sake, or if he was really only shielding himself. He had good reason, after all, not to want her to come into contact with the police. She had made no promises yet regarding what story she would tell if questioned.

In the dark warmth and quiet of Grandfather Rotham's backseat, Teagan sank gratefully into the soft leather. Sir had turned up the heater full blast, and she closed her eyes and buried herself under the blanket of his jacket, still wrapped around her. She didn't know or care what had ever become of her fur coat and handbag. It was an immense relief to be someplace where she could feel safe again.

Sir continued to surprise her with his considerate behavior, pulling her gently to his side so that her head rested against his shoulder. She was too exhausted, emotionally and physically, to protest—even had she wanted to, and she wasn't sure she did. He insisted she drink a calming glass of champagne, and she couldn't find the will to argue with that either.

The drink seemed to settle her churning thoughts, even as it made her drowsy. It was cozy and warm inside the car, with the thick flurries of white flakes swirling against the windows outside. She could've nuzzled up against Sir's broad shoulder and fallen asleep then and there. But he wouldn't allow it.

"You've yet to give me an answer," he said softly, brushing a loose tendril of hair out of her face. Her elaborate hairdo was in shambles now, the trailing curls tumbling limply around her face and shoulders.

She murmured sleepily, "I wasn't aware there was a question."

"I didn't think I needed to voice it. It has to be on your mind. What happened tonight, all that you've learned about me... Will you keep my secrets?"

Teagan sighed. "I don't know. I'll think about it."

Surprisingly, he nodded acceptance. "I suppose that's about the most I have any right to expect from you right now. Only keep this one thing in mind while you're considering."

Teagan half expected some sort of threat or bribe to follow. That's what she felt sure she would've gotten from the old Sir. But tonight's Sir offered an explanation, something she'd rarely known him to bother with. "I have no choice in what I am," he said. "No matter how deeply I loathe the beast controlling me—and I do very much—it's beyond my power to rid myself of him. You must believe me when I say I've tried. I've struggled to find a solution ever since this evil curse befell me."

Teagan lifted her head. "Then you weren't born a—"

"A werecat?" he finished for her with a bitter smile. "No. This change only took place a few months ago. I've put a lot of thought and effort into discovering how it happened and how I can reverse it."

"All those medical and science books…" Teagan said, remembering the bookshelf in the red bedroom of his apartment. "You were trying to research your condition."

"And the horror novels lining the shelves. I'm sure you noticed those too. I hoped I might find some grains of truth embedded in fiction. But it was a wasted effort. Nothing I learned could help me. A cure seemed beyond my reach. The best I could do was to piece together what happened and who was responsible for it."

"Someone was responsible? You mean it didn't come about on its own?"

"Indeed, there was a cruel human mind behind my transformation. One dark and vindictive." He hesitated before plunging into his story. "About a year ago, I foreclosed a loan on a business I had formerly supported that had long been going under. It had never turned in any profits and I had lost faith in its object. It was a scientific establishment being run in the backwoods of Vermont."

Teagan's heartbeat quickened as a horrible sense of foreboding awoke within her. Could this scientific establishment have been run by a man named Dr. Green? "Tell me more." She hoped her tone gave nothing away.

"The man who ran the business claimed he was working on great scientific discoveries that would revolutionize the modern medical profession. One project I remember he was especially fanatical about was the development of a serum that would lend renewed strength to the body and add years to the life of its user." He hesitated. "It sounded good at first. But the problem was for all this man's talking, his business showed no results. He was losing money, and the bank couldn't keep up his loan indefinitely when he was unable to pay. We foreclosed on him. And that's when the letters started to arrive."

"The threatening note," Teagan said. She tried to keep her voice steady. "The one I found in your drawer."

"That's right. This man, who I quickly came to recognize as slightly unbalanced, began deluging me with written attacks. They came to my office, they were mailed to my home. Phone calls too. I couldn't get away from him. Finally, I threatened to call the police, and that seemed to stop him. At least for a while. I thought I would hear no more from him." He stopped.

"And?" Teagan prodded anxiously.

"And then, one day, I was at work in my office when a package arrived for me in the mail. Kat usually opens my mail, or one of the other office assistants. But that day, by whatever twist of fate, it was me who opened that small, brown box."

Teagan leaned forward. "What was inside it?"

"Nothing," he said simply. "It was empty. Empty save for a tiny needle cleverly affixed to the top flap, which I couldn't have helped but prick my finger on in opening. I was puzzled by its meaning at first. It was just a little prick, a faint stinging sensation working up my hand, and then nothing. I wasn't too worried about it. I went home and forgot the incident... Until the first full moon, until my first transformation. Now, of course, I've come to accept the truth."

"That you were a victim of a crazy man's experimental serum?" she asked, horror stealing over her. Her secret communications with Dr. Green suddenly took on a whole new light. No wonder the man wanted her to record Sir's every move. She was a part of this experiment too, as an unwitting observer, documenting the subject's behaviors. She just hadn't understood before what she was supposed to be observing.

He shrugged. "I'm not sure if he meant it to have the effect that it did. Possibly it was only an experiment on his part. However, there can be no doubting why he chose me as his subject. He had threatened vengeance on me often enough. But when it came it was worse than anything I could have imagined. So now you know my secrets. Or at the least, the worst of them. Care to trust me with yours?"

"Secrets?" she asked, startled.

"Come on," he said. "You haven't kept quiet about your past all this time for nothing. Clearly, you haven't wanted to talk about who you used to be, or what brought you to take up residence on the city streets. Up until now, I've been too polite to ask."

"You? Polite?" she asked, disbelievingly. "Somehow I can't picture it. Anyway, I've hardly been secretive. Not everyone cloaks their personal lives in shadow as carefully as you do. If I've kept myself to myself it's because I hadn't imagined you'd be interested."

"I'm interested in anything that concerns you," he said lowly.

Suddenly aware of his nearness, a shiver shot through Teagan, but it was a hot, tingling feeling, not an unpleasant sensation. "There's—there's little to tell," she said, trying to conceal a sudden awkwardness. She was never shy. Where was this coming from?

"I had a lousy life and a screwed up family. Throw in a huge number of personal mistakes as well, and it's easy to see how things got out of hand. I hated my life, and I imagined that escaping the place I'd lived and everyone I knew would somehow fix all of my problems. I can see now it was stupid not to have a plan, but at the time I was feeling desperate. I threw the past behind me and ran toward the future. A few weeks later saw me with no money, no job, and too much pride to return to my mom and stepdad."

"So you thought a more dignified alternative would be to live out of trashcans and sleep in dirty alleyways?"

"You're laughing at me." She frowned. "Look, I knew you wouldn't understand—"

"Never underestimate what I might understand," he interrupted. "After all, if there's one thing we've both proved, you can never tell what secrets are hidden inside a person." He changed the subject. "So you never saw your family again. Think you ever will?"

"I—I don't know." She shook her head. "Listen, I know I said I didn't mind talking about it, but I guess it sort of still bothers me a little. Do you mind if we don't go into the details?"

She hadn't been aware she was wringing her hands in her lap until he slipped his hand over hers. "If it's difficult for you, we won't talk about it."

It seemed like a good time to change the subject. She said, "Speaking of families, I guess this is my opening to tell you. Your grandfather just sort of tried to enlist me, or bribe me or something, earlier. He wanted me to spy on you."

To her surprise, he laughed. "Don't worry. He does that to every woman I date."

The sense of relief she felt was enormous. "Really? Then he won't do anything horrible if I don't—"

"Don't report back to him? Of course not." He laughed again. "He's a bit devious, but he's not evil. He senses something's wrong, and he just wants to protect me."

It was a relief to know she didn't need to worry about the old man. Still, there were too many other burdens on her mind for the lightening of this one to leave her fully content. She tackled the next awkward problem.

"Does this mean I'm keeping my job? You know, as your doorkeeper? It'll be a lot easier now that I know the truth."

His expression became troubled, distant. "I don't know," he said. "I don't know how any of this is going to end."

Teagan became aware the car had pulled to a stop outside her apartment building. She felt strangely reluctant to step outside when Sir climbed out and held the door for her. The snow still drifted down, clinging to her hair and dropping cold, wet kisses anywhere it met her bare skin. Teagan gathered her trailing skirt to keep it off the soggy sidewalk.

"Well," she said softly. "I guess this is it. See you." She walked backward toward the looming doors, waiting for him to return the words. He never did. She watched him, watching her, until the pale flurries formed a thick curtain between them and his dark form standing on the curb dissolved into nothing more than an indistinct shadow.

Then through the swirling flakes and the surrounding gloom her ears caught the words, "Goodbye, Teagan."

Chapter 29

THAT NIGHT, TEAGAN LAY AWAKE, listening to the soft rustling noises of the mice scratching at the floor under her bed and the faint *drip, drip,* of the leaky showerhead behind the bathroom curtain. The lamp beside her bed was on, for she knew this was one night she wouldn't be able to sleep without it. In fact, trying to sleep at all seemed like a useless gesture even with the comfort of the lamp's yellow glow.

Her eyes tracked the progress of a large, black bug crawling busily across the ceiling over her bed, but its presence didn't bother her. A hundred bugs wouldn't have concerned her. Not tonight. Her thoughts were far away, reliving over and over the events of the past evening. She never did find any sleep that night.

At one point, she arose and turned on the lamp beside her bed. Reaching inside the bottom drawer of her nightstand, she drew out the letter she had received from Dr. Green. Was it only a few days ago she had first opened it with shaking hands? Now she removed the letter from its envelope and examined it more carefully than ever before.

A part of her couldn't help noting with relief there were no hidden needles affixed to anything. Not that she really believed she could have missed something like that before, but still... She read through the letter, looking for any sign, any clue that should have told her from the beginning she was dealing with a madman.

But there was nothing out of the ordinary. Nothing any more out of the ordinary than this whole business had been anyway. Eventually, she gave up and stuffed the letter back into its hiding place.

She went back to bed for a while, but it was no good. The clock showed it was just past five in the morning when she abandoned all thought of getting any rest and arose to dress. As she sat on the edge of the bed, pulling on her boots, she considered her situation. She knew it was a cold, crazy hour to go out, but she had no choice. After all of last night's explanations and admissions, she had one final confession to make. Besides, there was still a burning question she needed put to rest—one only Sir knew the answer to.

Dragging on her jacket and twisting a thick blue scarf around her neck, she caught a glimpse of her disheveled figure in the mirror. Her hair was uncombed, her clothing sloppy. Her face told the story of her sleepless night far better than any words could have. But none of it mattered. On a day like this, the last thing on her mind was appearances. She snatched up her purse and slipped out the door into the echoing stairwell.

Once she was outside the icy air was unexpectedly invigorating, washing away the drowsiness that had dragged at her before. Energy renewed, she decided a brisk walk to Sir's apartment was just the exercise she needed to shake away the last shadows of lost sleep and give her time to think over all she needed to say.

It wasn't yet light out, but the street lamps provided enough light for her to make her way by, and with the streams of traffic already crowding the streets she wasn't worried about walking alone in the dark. Besides, a hint of gray was touching the sky in the east, promising it wouldn't be long before sunrise. Her boots slogged through the melting snow, the passage of many feet over the sidewalk having already deteriorated the coat of pristine white to a churned bed of gray.

All of these details Teagan noted with a kind of detached awareness. Her thoughts were on the encounter ahead, on planning out her own words, and trying to anticipate his responses. Last night she had learned so much during that short car ride home. So much and yet so little. So focused had she been on the revelation of Sir's secret and on everything else that had just transpired that somehow she had never thought to seek the truth on a matter much closer to her heart.

Puffing out clouds of white breath, she treaded onward, shivering under the blast of the wind and shoving her frozen hands deeper into her pockets. Within her boots, her toes were little numb blocks of ice. Her nose and cheeks would be red and chapped by the time she arrived. She looked, she thought, much like the unkempt mess she had been the first time she visited Sir's apartment. Only this time she traveled there in a much different state of mind.

The fear was still there, the uncertainty at what lay ahead. But it was a different kind of fear this time. The fear of rejection. And the uncertainty wasn't over whether or not she was making the right decision, but whether or not the results would be all she hoped for.

Their time together last night, everything they had been through, had left her certain of one thing. She was in love with Sir. Hopelessly, maybe even pathetically, in love. But it was love just the same, and it was real. She had been wrestling with the notion for some time, denying to herself what should have been clear from the beginning. But all that denial, that internal turmoil had ceased the moment she saw Sir's life threatened, the instant she realized she might be about to lose him forever. Her heart still beat faster at the memory of the crazy gunman's weapon leveled right at Sir. She would've done anything just then, anything to save him. Even if it meant throwing her own life away.

That was how she understood the depth of the emotion burning within her. Surely that kind of devotion wasn't a whim, a flickering fancy that would be snuffed out by the first winds of hardship. She shook her head. No, her own feelings were clear enough to her now—ineradicably clear. It was Sir's emotions that left her in suspense.

Was his gentle behavior with her last night an

indication that he had some feelings for her as well? Or had he merely been exhausted by their ordeal, off his guard, and vulnerable to her questioning? Would today find him the same caring man he had been when he stood beneath the drifting snow and told her goodbye? Or would she find a transformed Sir waiting for her, the colder, more controlled stranger whose secrets kept her always at arm's length—who seemed eager that it should stay so?

All too soon, she found herself standing before the doors to Sir's apartment house. As she passed the doorman and rode the glass walled elevator up to the top floor, she asked herself if this would be the last time she ever made this trip. Would her declaration today, her admission of her feelings for Sir, ensure the end of their relationship? And what about her secret dealings with Dr. Green? Would he forgive her for those?

It was no good torturing herself with possibilities. Soon enough she would know everything. She steeled herself for the encounter ahead, uncertain whether to attribute the rising excitement in her to anticipation or dread. The elevator came to a stop and, with a *ding*, the doors drew open.

Cautiously, Teagan peered into the room before her. She hadn't been invited up here, she suddenly remembered. Maybe Sir was having one of his drinking bouts, or worse, was undergoing one of those bestial transformations he was cursed with. Then again, it was weeks before the next full moon, wasn't it? She should be safe enough. Even if she wasn't, she'd take her chances. With that decision firmly in mind, she stepped off the elevator and into the living room. The doors immediately closed behind her and as quickly as that, her one mode of escape vanished.

A single lamp illuminated the room with a soft yellow light, much like the last time she had been up here—the occasion where she had witnessed one of Sir's tortured dreams. She silenced the distracted thoughts that memory aroused and proceeded further into the room.

"Sir?" she called softly into the perfect stillness. "Anybody home?" Only the echoes of her own voice came back to meet her. "Hello?" she called more loudly.

Still nothing. She poked her head into the den to find it empty. The lingering warmth emanating from the now dark fireplace, however, suggested it couldn't have been long since someone had been in here. The room was in its usual order and there were no clues to suggest what had become of its last inhabitant.

She proceeded to the red bedroom next, that secret place which had once so filled her with terror when she awoke to find herself a prisoner there. It seemed a likely place to find Sir at this early hour. Only it too turned out to be empty. The bed didn't look as if it had been slept in, yet she was sure he had returned to this room, at least briefly, after the banquet last night. She knew it because the tuxedo he had worn lay thrown over the back of a chair, forgotten, and his shoes lay discarded nearby. The closet door stood open as if he had been inside recently, rummaging through his clothing, but there was no sign of him now.

Growing more and more confused, Teagan

checked the rest of the apartment, exploring rooms she had never before visited. By this time, she was fairly certain Sir wasn't in the apartment. He would have responded to her calls by now. And yet curiosity made her continue poking her head into the rooms. She'd never had free reign like this to explore every corner of the place. Somehow she felt Sir wouldn't mind under the circumstances.

In the end, she found herself standing before the closed door to the study. Everything about the sturdy red door's silent, imposing appearance discouraging her from prying into whatever secrets it concealed. Sir's old instruction against opening the door rang loudly in her head. Yet she knew the secret of this room now. She was aware of its purpose. Surely, that made it a secret no more.

She tried to imagine what his response would be if he learned she had entered that room without his permission. Somehow, she couldn't picture it being anything too terrible anymore. She no longer feared the wrath of Sir—not now that she knew what was behind it. Respect for the man's privacy made her hesitate, but curiosity drove her to stretch out a hand anyway, and give the knob a turn.

She had expected to find it locked as usual, had thought she would have to go into the den and remove the brass key from its hiding place beneath the silver box. But to her surprise, at her experimental twist to the knob, the door swung open easily, revealing a dimly lit interior.

Chapter 30

CAREFULLY, TEAGAN ADVANCED INTO THE room. She had already been informed as to the room's true use. Nevertheless, she was startled at the wreckage before her. The walls were battered and scored by long gouges, the deep marks of a frenzied creature's claws as it raked them over the plaster. The furniture was overturned, and much of it smashed to bits so that some pieces were almost unrecognizable as former chairs, tables, and a sofa.

There was a desk too. The heavy oak monstrosity sat in the center of the room, a lone, sturdy island surrounded by chaos. The once smooth wood had been chewed and clawed, the drawers ripped out and dashed into splinters, but the strong frame remained standing, impervious to the abuse. Atop this desk rested the room's one light source, a cracked lamp with a missing shade. Teagan could imagine him coming into this room recently and digging it carefully out of the rubble, to set out for her. She didn't know how she knew that the light had been left for her. Somehow she just did.

Approaching the bald lamp, her gaze fell to what lay beneath the pool of its light. A single sheet of clean, white paper. She had become familiar enough with Sir's handwriting over the past weeks to recognize his writing scrawled across the page. With trembling hands, she lifted the note and brought it up to the light.

Dear Teagan,

If you are reading this, then you have come, as I knew you would. You have more questions, to which you hope to find the answers for here. Once you arrived, of course, you were unable to resist the chance to look in on the forbidden.

She sensed the humor in the words. He wasn't angry, but amused by her prying.

She read on.

I want you to see this room. I want one person in this world to know the truth, and I have chosen you as that person. From the beginning I've trusted you above all others, have risked more to your care. Now, daily it grows more and more important to me to show you who I really am. I need you to see the results of my curse with your own eyes, so you can fully understand, perhaps for the first time, what you have involved yourself in.

Why so urgent, this sudden need to reveal my secret? I've asked myself that many times. Maybe it's a test. Maybe I want to see if you can accept me for who I am, or if you'll run screaming away like any sane woman would. If that's the object, then my test becomes a punishment for us both.

Teagan struggled to follow his meaning. *...a punishment for us both.* Was he implying to lose her would pain him? Surely not. She tried to silence her hopes. Sir wasn't the sort of man capable of returning feelings like hers. She mustn't allow herself that assumption. The note continued.

> *My desperation to learn your response, unfortunately, will have to wait. I have pressing business that must be completed if I'm ever to harbor any hopes toward a normal life...with you. Don't try to follow me. You mustn't interfere in any way. I will succeed or fail alone.*

Her eyes dropped to the signature, which was signed simply: *Sir.*

Teagan's mind reeled as she dropped the scrap of paper. He spoke of learning her response, of living a life with her. Did that mean what her trembling hopes whispered it could? Or was she somehow reading too much into it? No. *A normal life...with you.* There was no way to misread that.-

She looked around the room with its tattered furniture and clawmarked walls. Could she accept him for what he was? She didn't have to think about it. She had already, almost from the moment she learned the truth. Nothing could make her draw back from Sir.

With shaking hands, she switched off the lamp and stumbled from the room, drawing the door closed behind her. What urgent business did Sir have that had taken him away—both his absence from the apartment and his warning against following him suggested a journey of some sort. Where had he gone? Where could he possibly hope to find a cure for his transformations? If, indeed, a cure was what he had hinted at. Why else would he drop everything and disappear so quickly?

It seemed clear something had happened last night that had persuaded him he could no longer live in this state. Maybe it was the attack of that crazy man. Maybe it was his own feelings—if she dared believe it—for her that had inspired him to seek help. Either way, he was gone now and with him any opportunity of learning where or why he went. Was this it then? Was she expected to simply sit back and wait for whatever length of time to pass before she could hope to know the truth?

Then it struck her. She scrambled to Sir's bedroom, dropped to her knees before the dresser, and dragged out the bottom drawer. Rummaging through the garments, it only took her a few seconds to dig out that fateful letter, a scribbled warning from a crazy man, a scientist who was being forced to give up his studies… one who hovered on the edge of a unique discovery.

She quickly found the letter wasn't there. Not surprising. Where Sir was going he would need the return address on the envelope.

She left the apartment.

Don't follow me. Sir's instructions tugged at her during the elevator ride down to the lobby, but she refused to pay them heed. She couldn't let him go to face that lunatic alone. This wasn't a question of choice, but a matter of what must be done.

Unreasonable as she knew it was, she couldn't

shake the feeling her secret betrayal with Dr. Green left her at least partially responsible for whatever confrontation might take place between them. At this point, she hardly knew which man was more in need of her protection. Already, Sir had a long head start on her, if he had left last night. The thought urged her to haste. There was no time for anything, save one important errand...

She hopped in a cab, which she rode to the local branch of NationBank. In the car, she wrote on the back of a paper receipt from her purse, scribbling a hasty note she then dropped off with the red-haired Kat at the bank. She hadn't time for long explanations. Sir's shrewd grandfather would put it together for himself. At least, she hoped he would.

Settled back in the seat of the taxi again, Teagan closed her eyes a moment and wished she had gotten a little more sleep the night before. She had a long journey ahead of her and no idea what lay waiting at the other end of it. She was going to the bus station and then to Vermont.

Chapter 31

TEAGAN LEANED HER FOREHEAD AGAINST the cold windowpane and looked out at the gray scenery whizzing by. She had always imagined the countryside outside the city to be a fresh and colorful world full of wildlife and greenery. Instead, the passing landscape was drab and unwelcoming, gripped in winter's fist just as tightly as the city had been. Sleet beat a steady drumming against the glass. The cars passing in the other lane drove with yellow headlights beaming in the middle of the day and moved at a dismal crawl.

Still, watching the passing traffic and scenery was a pleasanter pastime than studying the interior of the dirty bus, or meeting the shifty eyed glances of her fellow passengers. She kept her purse clasped firmly in her lap and tried to make it clear by her expression she wanted no communication with the strangers around her. She didn't care that many of them might be perfectly nice people, or that she was probably coming off as rude and unfriendly. She had more pressing matters on her mind and these consumed her thoughts.

Six hours since she had left the city. How much of a head start on her did Sir have? Doubtless, he'd chosen a faster mode of transportation. But maybe he would make stops along the way. Maybe he would sleep in a hotel somewhere overnight? Surely if she traveled throughout the night, she would eventually catch up to or even pass him. She wanted, no, needed to arrive before him. Yet he seemed to have every advantage. An earlier start, faster conveyance… And he knew where he was going. She didn't have anything more to go on in the way of directions than the name of the business she sought and the town and state in which it was located. She regretted not having had the foresight to stop by her apartment for the envelope containing the full address.

She bit back an overwhelming sense of hopelessness. She hadn't come this far to give up. Sir needed her, whether he knew it or not, and she wouldn't fail him. Who knew what sort of dangers his enemy was capable of? Anyone unhinged enough to plant a needle tipped with experimental serum in the way of an innocent man was crazy enough to do anything. No, one way or another, she would be there to stop things from going too far. She would make her destination in time.

Holding firm to that determination, she leaned back against the seat and closed her eyes. It would be wise to catch up on her sleep now while she had the opportunity. She had a hunch she was going to need her strength.

Late-afternoon of the next day found her seated on a lonely bench at a rundown bus stop. A rust covered sign nearby read *Welcome to River Falls*. It didn't add a population number, but looking around her now, Teagan estimated it at about five hundred. Maybe that was a slight exaggeration on her part. Maybe it was coming so newly from the city that made this rural town seem like nothing more than a tiny dot on the map.

Yet the place was big enough somebody had thought it merited its own bus stop, and she could see that just a little ways farther down the road, it also boasted a diner. The rumbling ache in her empty stomach suggested that would be a likely stop in the near future. She hadn't seen a sandwich—or a clean restroom either for that matter—all day.

Still, she hesitated. Glintwood Options had been the name of the place Dr. Green had spoken of in the letter to Sir. Would anyone here know how she could find this place or the man who ran it?

Momentarily, the enormity of her task rose up to smother her in a sense of hopeless panic, but she quickly squelched the feelings. Right now, she needed a clear head and a fixed plan.

An hour later, she sat huddled over a small table, enjoying the comforting warmth of Donna's Diner, as she bit into a mouthwatering pastry. In truth, it was late in the day for doughnuts and this one might have been considered slightly stale at any other time. But it had been a day and a half since her last real meal and at this point, her stomach would have thought banana peels were the tastiest morsels it had ever encountered. Besides, she'd eaten out of enough garbage cans in her day to appreciate anything that was served up on a clean plate.

She shoved the last bite into her mouth and dusted the crumbs from her hands. Hunger abated at last, she glanced around at her fellow diners: an ancient man with a small dog at his feet and a newspaper spread across his table, and a pair of middle-aged fishermen with their poles propped between their table and the wall.

"Excuse me," she hailed the passing waitress. "Could I get a little more coffee?"

The gray-haired woman obligingly paused to fill Teagan's cup from the coffeepot in her hand. Her name tag read *Betta*. Maybe there really was no Donna.

"Um, I was wondering," Teagan hurried, as the waitress was about to leave, "if you could give me some directions. I'm new around here, and I'm looking for a friend who came here looking for a different friend..."

She was making a mess of it. She started over. "I need to find this place, Glintwood Options. I think it's some sort of business or—"

"Sure, sure, I know it," the waitress interrupted with an impatient glance toward her other customers. "Dr. Mortimer Green," she put a sarcastic inflection on the doctor part, "owns the Glintwood property, and he's a legendary nut job in these parts. Grab a pen, though, honey, 'cause this ain't gonna be short."

Teagan dug a pen from her purse and snatched up one of the napkins scattered across the table. "Go ahead, please."

The diner had a payphone in the back and a battered old phone book Teagan used to look up the small town's single taxi service. A car of her own would've made things so much simpler. After making the call, she returned to her table and sat a few more minutes sipping coffee from her steaming mug. For a short while, she allowed her mind to wander to Sir and exactly what he planned to do to make this Dr. Mortimer Green right his wrong. Could the man provide a cure for Sir's condition? Would he be willing to? And most worrisome of all, what would Sir do if he refused?

With thoughts like these, it was a relief when her ride arrived. She had to get to Glintwood Options and find Dr. Green before Sir did.

Chapter 32

L ONG BEFORE THE TAXI DROPPED her off in front of the tall chain link fence surrounding the Glintwood property, Teagan began to question her resolve. The road here had been a long and rutted dirt path, twisting snakelike, through a thick forest of pines. It was a wild, lonely looking place, abounding in wildlife, but with little sign of human habitation save in the crude, endless road that wound through its heart.

Now her last link with civilization was driving off in a trail of exhaust, leaving her standing alone with the looming forest at her back. The prospect before her looked no more inviting. There was something formidable about the sprawling eight foot fence she faced and the multitude of padlocks all over its closed entrance. It was far from impassible. In fact, with only one or two attempts, she managed to leap up and grab the edge of the fence. After that, it was simple enough to clamber over the top and drop to the ground on the other side. Nevertheless, the idea that whoever owned this property was very eager to keep visitors out wasn't lost on her.

Now that the barrier of the fence was behind her, Teagan looked around to see what she had gotten herself into. Before her spread a vast, empty space, dotted with more pines. The long fence didn't end the forest, but merely interrupted it, cutting straight through the trees, so that the area encircled by the chain link appeared nearly as wild as that outside. The dirt driveway led up to the only manmade structure in sight: a large warehouse-like building made of sheet metal and random scraps of construction material. Not quite what she'd expected of Glintwood Options.

A careful survey of the premises revealed no sign of anyone stirring in the open. If Dr. Mortimer Green was around, he was keeping to himself inside the building. Then again, who was to say he lived here? Just because he ran his laboratory, or whatever it was, from in there, didn't mean he hung out here all the time. She wished she'd thought to ask that waitress about his home address. Ah well, it was no use worrying about it now. Surely if she poked around a little on the property she could find something of use.

Her initial plan as she crossed the distance to the warehouse wasn't to try and find a means of secret entrance. Merely to explore the property and to see what she could make of it from close range. Once she rounded the corner of the building, however, any such cautious ideas were instantly cast aside. For there, parked at back of the warehouse, was a long shiny blue car.

There was nothing to say it wasn't Dr. Green's car, of course, she rushed to assure herself. After all, the man had to get way out here somehow. And then she saw the license plate bore the name of a rental company. And it wasn't a Vermont plate. No, like it or not, Dr. Green had a visitor, and she had a pretty good idea of who it was. So much for beating Sir to the punch.

Clamping down on the emotions inside her threatening to stir out of control, Teagan forced herself to think coolly, rationally. Even if it was Sir in there with the doctor, it didn't mean anything violent had happened, or would happen. Sir was a reasonable man, and surely this Dr. Green would be open to negotiations. He must see how wrong what he had done to Sir was.

And yet in the back of Teagan's mind loomed another face. She couldn't forget the crazy glint in the eye of the gunman who had threatened her only two nights ago. She had seen insanity before, had been close enough to madness to recognize there were people in the world who were unbalanced, and dangerously so. Was Dr. Green one of those? She hoped not, for his own sake. There had been enough violence already. *Please let him give Sir what he needs and just let him go*, she prayed.

But even as the thoughts passed through her mind, she was creeping in closer to the warehouse. She had no intention of risking all she had come to hold dear on Dr. Mortimer Green's sanity—which had already proved questionable. Sane people didn't usually go around affixing needles to surprise packages.

She clung to the dark tree line until she was near enough to the car parked in back of the building to make a break into the open. It was only a short sprint across open ground before she was ducking down in the shadow of the vehicle, and yet by the time she got there, her heart was thudding against her ribs. She wasn't used to this kind of thing.

Keeping low, she raised herself just enough to peer in through the car windows. The backseat was empty. But lying in the passenger seat was a full-length dark coat—one she instantly recognized as belonging to Sir. He had been wearing that coat on the night they first met. So. It was settled. She peered around the car toward the silent warehouse. The moment she knew Sir had gone into that place, she also knew that she couldn't allow him to face whatever lay ahead alone. This Dr. Green seemed a dangerous man.

One way or another, she had to get inside. Announcing her presence was out of the question. If Sir was in trouble in there, it wouldn't do him any good for her to come barging into the middle of it. She had to think clearly. Had to form a plan. And yet every second that ticked by as she crouched here thinking was another second Sir's life could be in danger.

She glanced overhead. How much time had she wasted already? The sun was nothing more than a fiery blaze on the horizon now. Stars dotted the darkening sky here and there, and a pale sliver of moon was suspended among them. Not a full moon, she noted with relief. At least they didn't have that to add to their worries.

Returning her attention to the problem at hand, something about the warehouse caught her attention. Why hadn't she noticed it before? There was a heavy tin door, something like a garage door, in the back of the building, and this was cracked about a foot above the ground. Why would the garage door be left open?

Almost without thinking about it, she found herself inching forward, abandoning the shield of the car to cross open space once more. It seemed an eternity but could really have been only a matter of seconds before she left the open ground behind her and pressed herself up flat against the side of the warehouse. Dropping cautiously to one knee, she lowered her face down to the crack at the bottom of the door. The darkness inside afforded her a limited view of a patch of concrete floor. Nothing else.

It seemed too easy. Nevertheless, it was the only secret entrance that offered itself. She'd be a fool to pass it by. Lowering herself to the ground, she slithered silently on her belly beneath the edge of the door. There was barely clearance enough for her to make it, her back scraping lightly against the tin above.

The concrete floor was icy cold, but she didn't scramble immediately to her feet once inside. It was as dark as a moonless night in here and she had no idea what sort of place she had just entered. She had to proceed with caution. And so, she lay motionless for some minutes, waiting for her eyes to adjust to the dimness.

Gradually she began to pick out shapes in the

dark. Looming towers lined one wall—she quickly recognized them to be tool chests. Other odd shapes hung suspended from the ceiling. An old bicycle, a pair of skis. A tire was propped against the near wall alongside an exercise bike with a missing seat. This room seemed pretty much like any other garage she had ever seen the inside of. Dr. Green apparently made this warehouse his home then, or at least his shed for storing junk.

A soft rustle, coming from somewhere very near captured Teagan's attention. She stiffened. Rats? But no, in the dimness, she could vaguely make out one more shape resting a handbreadth away. And then she knew why the door had been left cracked. Curled up, bare inches from her, was the most immense Rottweiler Teagan had ever seen, a vicious looking creature of black hide and bulky muscle. And she had awakened him.

Staring into the blazing yellow eyes glowing back at her, Teagan froze.

Chapter 33

VEN AS TEAGAN'S MIND RACED to find a way out of her predicament, she wondered why the animal simply lay motionless, staring at her. Why didn't it attack already? Or raise an alarm? Any second now, she should hear a low, threatening growl begin rumbling in the back of its throat.

But the dog was strangely silent. If anything, its large eyes were questioning. Why, it seemed to be asking, was this stupid stranger crawling across the floor like a cockroach?

"Easy, puppy," Teagan crooned, moistening her lips. "That's a nice, big fellow. You wouldn't hurt me, would you?"

The dog cocked its massive head to one side. A strange thumping sound broke the stillness and it took Teagan a moment to understand it wasn't the thud of her heart, but the sound of the dog's tail wagging against the floor. Relief washed over her. This watchdog was a teddy bear.

"That's right," she whispered reassuringly, "I'm

nobody bad. You don't eat me, and I won't eat you. How's that?"

For answer, the dog stretched out its neck and lowered its heavy head.

"What, you want your ears scratched?" she asked, tentatively obliging. It felt a little like petting a huge bear, but the dog seemed gentle enough. Once she was satisfied she wasn't in immediate danger of being devoured, she took another look around at her surroundings. There had to be a way into the main building from here. And then she saw it—a narrow doorway at the far side of the room.

Slowly, she crawled to her feet. She needn't have worried on the dog's account. Already satisfied with her brief stroking, he laid his nose down between his paws again and let her go.

It wasn't easy, working her way in the dark around the piles of junk that stood between her and the door. When she reached it, she tried the knob and the door opened easily. Teagan released the breath she'd been holding. If it had been locked, she didn't know what her next step would have been. Carefully, she pressed one eye up against the cracked door.

Her limited view afforded her a glimpse of the interior of the warehouse. The florescent lighting high in the ceiling was dim, but at least it was there. Beneath its flickering light, Teagan made out a vast space of concrete floor, cluttered by stacks of crates and various debris that looked like trash to her. Having seen the warehouse from the outside, Teagan knew it to be even larger than this, but apparently parts of it were sectioned off into separate rooms.

The wooden rafters overhead stored still more boards, boxes, and long sheets of metal, resting longways across the ceiling beams. The overall affect was one of an immense open space that had been crowded with so much debris there was scarcely walking space between the piles. At least, Teagan thought, this might simplify her attempts to avoid notice.

When her preliminary search revealed no one else in the room, she inched the door open just far enough to squeeze out. Then she made a stealthy rush to duck behind the nearest stack of wooden boxes. Once she was out of the open, she relaxed a little. From her hiding place, crouched behind the pile of crates, she peered around the room. If anyone else were here, they too must be hiding as she did. She wasn't sure if that was a comforting thought or not. Meeting up with Sir would be all right; she wanted to intercept him anyway. On the other hand, running into the mysterious Dr. Green in this eerie atmosphere would probably give her a heart attack.

Straining her ears, she tried to catch the slightest sound to hint that another person lingered nearby. From somewhere, she picked up the small, scratching sound of an insect skittering across the bare floor. Much louder was the occasional creak of the tin roof overhead as it groaned in the wind.

What was that? Teagan pricked up her ears. Was it her overeager imagination, or had she heard the drone of men's voices in the distance? As silently as possible, she moved closer to the direction the sound emanated from. This meant abandoning her temporary shelter behind the crates, but she hardly missed it. There was such a litter of debris scattered around her, she was well screened from view in any direction.

Unfortunately, that also meant she couldn't see who was doing the talking. And there was talking. The voices, once a soft buzz, were growing more distinct as she approached. But there was an annoying muffled quality to the deep tones that prevented her from making out the words. She realized the speakers were in another room, talking from behind one of these tin walls.

Finally, she could see the doorway letting into the other room. The door was open slightly, but from her present vantage point, she couldn't see in. If she could get at it from another angle… Cautiously, she crept nearer, moving from one shielding hill of debris to the next, until finally she was hiding in the shadows just outside the door. Her view was still limited to one corner of the room.

Here she could see a metal work desk, laden with test tubes and all sorts of other instruments she didn't know the uses of, shoved up against the far wall. Beside it was a cracked, dusty window overlooking the dark pine forest outside. She could see nothing of the room's inhabitants, save their shadows stretched across the floor.

"I didn't come to bribe you." Teagan's heart leapt in recognition as Sir's voice rang out angrily from the next room. "I won't pay you to undo what should never have been done in the first place."

"Do you think I want money?" The voice that answered was oddly steady, in light of the fact that an argument seemed to be underway between the two. If the speaker returned any of Sir's anger, his soft tone didn't reveal it. He continued, "No, my days of relying on you and your bank for support are over, my self-important friend. Do you want to know why? Shall I let you in on my little secret?"

He suddenly appeared into view, this other man, moving to the desk in the corner. His back was toward the door, so Teagan could make out nothing more of his features than a short, stocky frame and a balding head with a fringe of gray hair. He didn't look dangerous, this Dr. Mortimer Green. His voice and easy manner lacked the signs of madness Teagan had come to expect. Everything about him seemed ordinary.

He reached into one of the desk's drawers and withdrew something. "Look here," he said, conversationally. "The serum for a certain experiment. Already tested, already proved." He held the object, a syringe, up for viewing before replacing it in the drawer. "And what's this?" he continued, selecting another syringe. "The antidote. Also quite positively proved. But it's not for you, no." He laid the second syringe atop the desk where it lay temptingly in full view.

As he turned back to Sir, his face came into view. It was the round, pink-cheeked face of a middle-aged man who, aside from his black-rimmed glasses, bore no remarkable features. He looked like a gentle sort of man, somebody who collected butterflies and went on nature walks. He moved slightly and was no longer visible from Teagan's vantage point.

Reluctantly abandoning her shadowy hiding place, Teagan crawled stealthily across the floor, planning to press her face full against the door. Despite her careful movements, however, one boot scraped sharply against the concrete floor as she shifted. The resulting squeak echoed around the big warehouse. Teagan froze.

Inside the little room, both men turned at the sound. Caught in plain sight and clearly visible through the cracked door, Teagan could do nothing but observe the varied expressions crossing their faces. Sir's look was one of shock, swiftly replaced by anger. Beside him, Dr. Green scarcely even looked surprised.

"Teagan!" Sir exclaimed sharply. "What are you doing? How did you get in here?"

Shrugging sheepishly, she climbed to her feet. Now that she had been caught like a kid with her hand in a jar of sweets, it seemed silly to stay crouching on the cold floor. She crept abashedly through the doorway and into the smaller room.

"Why did you come?" Sir demanded. "I specifically told you in my note not to follow me!"

"I just wanted to help," Teagan offered. "I was afraid if I didn't come to stop things you might do something…hasty." Sir didn't look placated.

Dr. Green chose that moment to break into the conversation. "Teagan," he repeated thoughtfully. "I know that name."

Teagan's insides turned to ice. She'd hoped to avoid this. Why had she ever signed her real name to those letters? She shot the doctor a pleading glance but he didn't seem to get the message in her eyes. He continued speaking.

"You're the young lady who contacted me. The one who agreed to share our friend Mr. Rotham's secrets in exchange for the favorite reward of betrayers. Money." He offered a light chuckle.

"Teagan, what's he talking about?" Sir's voice was cool, neither accusing nor reproachful, merely requesting the truth. He would wait to learn it before he judged.

Teagan couldn't look at him. He deserved the truth. "I, um, sort of had this deal with Dr. Green where he was going to pay me a little bit to, er, spy on you. But I regretted the deal almost as soon as I agreed to it," she rushed on. "I was at the point of breaking it off and confessing everything to you many times, only—"

"Only you didn't," he finished for her. "I don't suppose there's any point in asking why you did it?"

Her eyes may as well have been glued to the toes of her boots. She offered an embarrassed shrug. "You know me," she said in a small voice.

He apparently got the idea. "Yes. Yes, I do. I know that greedy heart of yours has been to my advantage on more than one occasion. I suppose that it has finally turned to work against me is something I deserve." His tone became self-deprecating. "I've admitted to being many things over the years, but I never thought to call myself a trusting fool."

Teagan didn't know what to say. Her heart ached.

She could have told him she had only been observing him for a short time and that she had never passed on any particularly useful information. But it was the intent behind her actions that mattered. If she could see that, he would too. And so, she kept silent. Luckily for both of them, Dr. Green broke in at that moment.

"Come, Rotham, I think you're being a bit too hard on the girl. After all, she may have acted with mercenary intentions, but she was aiding in a scientific experiment. There are worse causes to join." He turned to Teagan. "But now as you see, young lady, our subject has become uncooperative and so, although our observation period didn't last as long as I would have liked, time has run out and the experiment approaches its end."

He turned suddenly on Sir. "I don't pity either of you. You, Mr. Rotham, impeded my progress. You hindered my science, and would have shut down my experiments altogether if you could, all in the name of greed. History is full of men such as you. Already wealthy and filled with their own worth, and yet they'll do anything to squash the last dime out of the little man. Even at the cost of scientific discovery, even at the cost of advancements to the human condition."

"You're crazy," Sir said bluntly, from across the room. Teagan followed his glance toward the syringe atop the desk. A single prick was all he needed to reverse his condition, yet this little man stood in his way. "What you've done to me wouldn't advance anyone's condition."

Strangely, Dr. Green merely smiled. "It all

depends, my belligerent friend, on how you look at the negatives and positives. Loss of your humanity, for example. Is that such a drawback really, when your strength is multiplied, and your life expectancy is ten times longer than that of an ordinary man? When you think of it in that light, I've done you a tremendous favor."

"So it was an act of generosity when you transformed me into a brutal beast who can't control his own actions?" Sir didn't sound grateful.

Both men seemed ready to dismiss Teagan's presence altogether.

Dr. Green shrugged. "I needed a healthy specimen and when you closed my loan, you made yourself an unwitting volunteer. It's not my fault if you haven't been bright enough to learn to control your transformations. With a little practice and concentration, you'll learn to transform at will."

"Thanks for the opportunity," Sir said dryly. "But I'm done being your test rat. Just give me the antidote." He strode toward the desk, but Dr. Green barred his way.

"Don't be a fool," the little man said, unruffled by Sir's intimidating figure looming over him. "You're in no position to demand anything. Do you imagine me quite helpless under your greater physical strength?"

Sir was undeterred. "I'll take my chances. Give me the syringe."

Dr. Green seemed not to hear him. An odd light had come into his eyes and his gaze was focused inward. His voice sounded hoarse, deeper as he asked, "Do you truly think you're one of a kind? A lone experiment?"

For the first time, Sir demonstrated uncertainty. "You tested yourself, didn't you?"

There was no need for response. Already the doctor's form was changing, growing. Teagan watched with fascinated horror as the gentle faced little doctor began warping into something less human. His height stretched until he towered over Sir. Fur quickly formed in patches across his face and exposed skin until there was nothing left of a man about him. His clothing tore and fell away, unable to accommodate his massive growth. Stomach roiling at the unnatural sight, Teagan couldn't help but turn her face away for a moment, and when she looked back, the transformation was complete. In place of the unassuming doctor, an immense brown coated grizzly bear towered over Sir.

Sir hadn't been inactive all this time. During the doctor's shape shifting, he had been inching around the growing creature, and now he made a sudden dash for the desk and the syringe that rested atop it.

With casual ease, the bear moved to stop him, swiping at him with a massive paw. What was a mere slap for a bear was a powerful blow to a man, and the force of it sent Sir reeling into the window beside the desk. Teagan gasped as the windowpane shattered and Sir tumbled out onto the ground below.

Chapter 34

THE BEAR SWIFTLY FOLLOWED SIR out the window, and both disappeared from Teagan's view. Temporarily frozen to the spot, it took her a second to react. Then, shaking away the sense of unreality that had taken hold of her, she crossed the room. Leaning out the window, she tried to see the forms of man and bear in the darkness. It was now full night and the faint glow of the moon overhead wasn't enough to illuminate the surrounding grounds.

Teagan located them by sound rather than sight. An animal roar ripping through the silence of the night and then the thundering of heavy footsteps moving toward the nearby stand of pines gave away their direction. Without thought for the prickly shards of glass or the short drop to the ground below, Teagan scrambled through the broken window and leapt down onto the grassy earth.

She was grateful for the level ground as she pursued the fleeing sounds of the others because coming from the light of the indoors, the world around her now seemed as black as the bottom of a well. Dimly, she saw the rising shapes of trees ahead. They were making for the forest bordering the edge of the property. Soon they would come up against the fence and there would be nowhere left to run.

She was forced to slow on entering the tree line. It was ever darker here and the looming shapes of pines, saplings, and fallen logs gave her pause. She would do Sir no good by stumbling in and breaking her neck. Carefully, she picked her way through the crowding vegetation. She could hear the sounds of a commotion up ahead. The noisy upheaval of undergrowth and the heavy cracking of sticks underfoot gave testament to some sort of struggle taking place among the trees. Teagan quickened her stride again. Eyesight finally growing accustomed to the dark, she made out two indistinct figures clashing in the small clearing she approached. Silvery moonlight filtered through the opening in the forest canopy above to illuminate the immense form of the grizzly bear just as it was charging toward the smaller figure of a man.

"No!" Heart leaping to her throat, Teagan let out a useless cry and raced toward them, knowing all the while that whatever happened would be over before she arrived.

Gaze fixed on the horrifying scene playing out before her, she gave no thought to where she placed her feet. She simply ran. Suddenly, a thick tree root protruding from the earth caught the toe of her shoe and dragged her down. For a terrible, frustrating instant, her face was buried in the mossy forest floor, and then she scrambled upright again.

Frantically searching the clearing ahead, she quickly identified and passed over the shape of the running bear. Where was Sir? He had disappeared. But in the place he had been a moment before, another now stood. Not a man, this time, but a massive, shadowy beast, resting on all fours, with a pair of blazing golden eyes that glowed beneath the moonlight. A cat, but like none she had ever seen. This creature was impossibly large for such an animal, more monster than beast. Rippling muscles stood out in bunches beneath his hide and sharp fangs gleamed pale in the night.

Sir, Teagan realized. So he had learned to control the transformation. He no longer needed a full moon to take on his beast form. She had no time to consider the implications of that. Everything was playing out too swiftly.

The bear was still barreling onward, and the panther stood directly in his path. The cat leapt forward an instant before the bear would have crashed into him, and they met in midair. Claws and teeth were bared on both sides and they tumbled to the ground with a *thud*, a writhing mass of snarling fur.

Holding her breath, Teagan watched the brown and black hides flash as they struggled across the forest floor, and waited to see who would come out on top. To her horror, it was the bear who was the first to regain his feet. With a roar, he slapped a heavy paw at the smaller animal, but the cat moved nimbly out of his path. Snarling, the puma dodged agilely in to snap at the bear's belly. He touched nothing but fur, however.

Bulky and lumbering as the bear was, it was surprisingly swift in its movements. In an instant, it turned the cat's attack to its advantage, slamming its weight down atop the body of the black beast. Immobilized, the puma was helpless to defend himself as the bear's sharp teeth descended to sink into the hide of his shoulder.

An agonized scream escaped the trapped animal, a mingled cry of hatred and helplessness. The bear tightened its grip on its victim's shoulder, shaking its head from side to side so that the smaller animal was whipped around like a rodent in the jaws of a cat. Crimson blood stained the night.

Teagan couldn't drag her eyes away from the terrible scene. When the bear finally released his prey, the puma was tossed limply against a nearby tree, his body hitting the trunk with a sharp cracking noise. Teagan expected to see him move no more, but after a brief moment, he crawled slowly to his feet again. His efforts were too slow, however, weakened by his injury.

Already his enemy was bearing down on him again, and this time Teagan sensed it was closing in for the kill. The cat must have sensed his end approaching as well, for he suddenly threw back his head, offered a wild, blood chilling scream to the moon, and turned to meet his attacker. Despite his obvious weakness, there was still a fiery defiance blazing from his glowing eyes.

The bear rammed into the cat, swiftly slapped down his attempts at defense and pinned him to the ground with one large paw. The cat's throat was exposed, open to the sharp teeth of the animal above. It would be an easy kill for the bear. The triumphant creature roared its victory, sank its long teeth toward the throat of its victim...

And was suddenly barreled into by another, smaller form, from behind. The Rottweiler from the warehouse. The dog was pitifully dwarfed alongside the bear, but it growled and snapped at the larger creature with a determined ferocity. Dodging before and behind the bear, the smaller animal somehow managed to be everywhere at once, worrying the bear to the point that it had to loosen its hold on the struggling cat to deal with this new threat. Yowling and snapping, the dog leapt onto the bear's back.

Teagan couldn't imagine how cruel Dr. Green must have been to make his own dog turn on him, but as she watched the cat wriggle free of the bear's grip, she could only feel gratitude toward the brave Rottweiler for darting to the rescue.

Now, however, it was clear the Rottweiler's role in this struggle was to be a short one. With a motion that was more annoyance than genuine fury, the bear tossed the dog easily from his back. Flying through the air, the smaller creature landed on the ground a little distance away, to lie motionless in the grass.

But the Rottweiler's efforts hadn't been wasted. During that brief moment of inattention, the bear had turned its back on the puma. The cat needed no more invitation than that. Seeming to call on hidden reserves of strength, he sprang onto the bear from behind, gleaming fangs sinking again and again into the bear's thick hide. Instantly, the bear's coat was stained with blood.

Letting out a cry of fury, the bear turned this way and that, trying to land a mighty paw on its enemy. But the cat was determined. More than that, he knew he was fighting for his life. Fangs sinking deeper into the flesh of his enemy, he hung on grimly, despite the bear's efforts to dislodge him.

Suddenly, he released his hold. Apparently expecting victory, the bear turned, prepared to destroy him. That was exactly the opportunity the cat had been awaiting. As soon as the bear turned, head raised, the puma dived straight into the embrace of its furry paws, teeth snapping toward the bear's throat.

Both werebeasts collapsed forward, tumbling to the ground, and Teagan's vision was momentarily blocked. All she could make out was a massive pool of blood-stained brown fur and beneath that, patches of wriggling, darker hide. There was a brief struggle, and then all was still. Silence descended over the clearing.

Teagan suddenly became aware she was trembling on the ground—that she hadn't yet arisen from her knees. With an effort, she started forward, stealthily approaching the motionless pair. As she moved nearer, there was an abrupt movement from the lifeless pile of fur. Teagan caught her breath, but it wasn't the bear that was stirring to life. From beneath its immense form, the panther wriggled free, crawling out from under the dead weight of the larger creature.

Teagan froze where she stood, gaze glued to the

glowing-eyed beast, anxiously examining the crimson stains marking the black hide. How strange it was to think inside the flesh of that mysterious wild beast beat the heart of the man she loved.

On noticing her presence, the cat stiffened, became absolutely still. And then his broad nose twitched, testing the scent of her on the evening air. Teagan searched for some sign of recognition in the depths of those glowing golden eyes. Some hint that Sir's darker, human gaze lurked behind them. For a brief instant she thought she sensed it, some wordless connection passing between them. She stepped forward, extending her hand.

And the spell was broken. Immediately, the yellow-eyed panther became just a wild creature again, retreating from her approach. Without another glance in her direction, he bounded off, disappearing through the gloom of the wood.

Teagan hesitated, glancing down at the dead grizzly bear at her feet. Nearby, the black Rottweiler was sitting up again and cautiously testing its legs. Teagan promised herself she would get the dog to a vet as soon as possible. She owed it that. But for now, there was a human life at stake.

Abandoning the clearing, she took off. Moving swiftly, she followed the path the puma had taken back out of the trees. She knew where he was headed.

Chapter 35

"**S**IR?" TEAGAN CALLED SOFTLY, STEPPING into the dim interior of the building.

In the distance she heard a faint rustle and the sound of a door creaking. There was no other response. Teagan followed the noises, climbing over and around the debris scattering the room. Stacks of crates loomed out of the darkness, stark shadows in the pale moonlight filtering in through overhead skylights.

Unfamiliar shapes and objects littered her path, making silent passage difficult, but she continued doggedly on, even when a blind stumble or a clumsy nudge sent a piece of debris rolling noisily across the floor or a stack of boxes collapsing with a *thud*. He had to know she was here. Even had she not announced her approach so loudly, he must surely guess that, at some point, he would be followed.

Suddenly, she heard a low groan. The sound was pained, weary—and very human. Had the transformation passed already? Could Sir be a man once more? She glanced toward the night sky, visible in patches through the overhead openings. Stars still twinkled above. It was still night. Too early for the transformation to pass. Then she remembered he apparently had some control over it now.

Again the groan. Her heart melted at the sound. He was hurt. Sir was hurt. Besides that, all other thoughts dissolved. She had to get to him. Scrambling over the mountain of obstacles in her way, she half ran, half stumbled in the direction of the noise.

There, just through the narrow doorway up ahead. The room the argument had occurred in. The sounds were coming from there. Heart hammering inside her breast, Teagan approached the cracked door. The heavy silence was interrupted only by the harshness of her rough breathing.

Crash. The sudden noise coming from beyond the door made her jump. Without thinking, she threw the door open and rushed into the room. Pale moonlight bathed the floor, filtering through the broken window in the far wall. The silver beam slanted across Sir's prone body collapsed across the floor. All traces of the puma were gone. In its place was simply a man—the man she loved—lying with deathlike stillness on the cold concrete.

Teagan swallowed and a harsh whisper escaped her lips, "No."

Rushing to his side, she dropped to her knees and gently rolled him over. Relief was like a douse of water smothering the burning fear inside her. He lived. His chest rose and fell rhythmically in the moonlight.

Teagan's joy was short lived. Blood stained Sir's

clothing, and his face was fixed in a mask of pain. He had brought his injuries back with him, upon reentering his human form. Having witnessed the duel of the werebeasts, Teagan knew his injuries were serious. Had she come all this way only to arrive in time to see him die? Hot tears burned in her eyes, threatening to spill over.

"Sir? Can you hear me? It's Teagan," she said.

At the sound of her voice, his eyelids shot open unexpectedly. "Get away from me." It was more of a pained gasp than a command but that made the words hit her all the more forcefully.

"What? No, I don't want to go. I came back to help you."

"Like you've helped me all along? Secretly plotting behind my back ever since—" His words cut off, interrupted by a spurt of coughing.

Teagan wondered fearfully about the extent of any internal damage. There was more going on here than just the cuts visible on his flesh. "Please. You mustn't talk right now. Least of all about this."

"Why not? Don't you want to make your apologies, ease your conscience a little before I die?" His tone bore a semblance of the old sarcasm she knew so well.

"I didn't race to your side for petty apologies," she said, swallowing hard. "I followed you out here to tell you that I'd made a mistake and that I...that I..."

"Let me guess. You've fallen in love with me." He looked like if he hadn't been suffering he would have laughed. "A bit late to go down that road, honey. I won't be hanging on long enough to add you to my will."

"I don't care about the money!"

"Since when?"

The question pulled her up short. He was right. When had she cared about anything but gaining advantages in life however she could? "People can change," she offered weakly.

He looked at her and, for the first time, seemed to register her emotions. He coughed again. "You're serious?"

"Of course I am. Dr. Green is dead and you're not much better off. Why would I be playing games at such a time?"

He seemed to consider her words for an instant. Then a sudden, sharp pain must have washed over him, for clinching his jaw, he fell silent, apparently concentrating all his strength on the inward agony.

Teagan didn't know how much longer she could stand this. "What's taking so long?" she wailed. "Help should've been here by now." She slipped her scarf from around her neck.

"Help?" he gritted. "Don't tell me you were silly enough to call in the police? Of all the fluff brained— Ow!" His lecture was interrupted by a howl as Teagan pressed the wadded scarf over the bleeding wound on his chest.

"No one called any police," she told him. "I left a message for your grandfather yesterday. He should be catching up to us anytime now, and when he does, hopefully, he'll have brought a little help. I didn't think I could do this on my own. Now keep still," she added, because a firm tone seemed to be the only way of getting through to him. "You're as stubborn in your death throes as you are in good health."

"Don't be ridiculous," he snorted, through gritted teeth. "Nobody's dying."

"That's not what you said a minute ago."

"A minute ago I was ready to give up. Now that I've wrung some sincerity out of you, I might have a reason to hang around awhile yet."

Teagan didn't know whether to laugh or cry. "Do you mean that? That you believe me? That I'm forgiven?"

The corner of his mouth twitched upward for a second. "Maybe…"

She sensed he was fading.

His next words confirmed it. "No more time for talk…I need…I just…" His voice trailed off and his eyes rolled closed. He was losing his battle to hang onto consciousness.

"Just need what?" Teagan asked urgently. "If there's something that can help, tell me what it is. Quickly."

His eyelids fluttered. "What I came for." He coughed. "Dr. Green invented a reversal serum. He told me but refused to give it to me. That's when—"

"That's when he transformed and you fought him. I know," she said. "What happened to the serum?"

"Desk." He pointed vaguely toward the metal counter beneath the window. "Still there."

Teagan reluctantly left his side and scrambled to the desk. There was an array of tubes and implements scattered across the workspace. But right away her eye fell on a long silver needle lying amid the clutter. It looked just like the ones they used in the doctor's office to draw blood, only, rather than blood, this one was filled with a clear, bubbly liquid.

"You're sure this is what you need?" she asked, kneeling, syringe in hand, at Sir's side.

"That's the one. He taunted me with the cure so close, and yet—"

"And yet he wouldn't give it to you," she finished. "What an evil man." Her thoughts were interrupted as outside, she heard the roar of a car's engine. Maybe several cars.

She wasn't the only one to have heard. "My grandfather," Sir observed. "Quick. Give me the shot before he gets here. He doesn't need to know all the details."

"Okay." Against her better judgment, Teagan complied, moving the needle to hover over his bicep, where the doctors always did it.

He shook his head, grabbing her wrist. "No," he gritted. "Heart. Faster that way." He weakly guided her hand to his chest.

Teagan poised the needle just over the skin. And then she hesitated, a sudden thought striking her. "What if this reversal serum saps the last life out of you? What if the strength of the cat is all that keeps you holding on?"

The corner of his mouth tugged up in a half smile. "Don't worry. I've got something much more powerful than that to hold me up." His dark eyes were unexpectedly soft. "I've got you, haven't I?" He lifted a tender hand to stroke her cheek.

Despite the uncertainty of their situation, a ray of warmth and hope shot through Teagan. "You meant what you said in your note, didn't you?" she asked quietly. "About us? A life together and all that."

He raised a brow. "I see I wrote too much of my heart into that letter. I should've saved it for a more romantic moment. A man doesn't like to make such proposals lying on his back in a pool of his own blood."

"You couldn't have chosen a better time or place," Teagan said truthfully, knowing that until this very instant, she would have been unprepared.

"I guess that says something about our strange relationship to date, doesn't it?" He tried to laugh and, instead, gave a groan at the pain the effort cost him.

"Oh no." Teagan bent over him. "Is it growing worse?"

He looked up into her eyes. "Much worse," he said softly. And then he raised a hand to the back of her head and pulled her face gently down to his. It was a slow kiss, a tender one. This was a touch Teagan could respond to with her whole heart.

"I think I like you this way," she said softly when it was over.

"What way? Bleeding to death?"

She gasped, starting upright. "Oh my gosh! You almost made me forget! We've got to get help in here and do something about these wounds."

"All in good time. The shot first," he reminded her.

"All right then." With shaking hands, Teagan raised the needle and poised it above his chest. She wasn't sure if she could do this.

In the distance she heard a sharp *bang*, the sound of one of the metal doors to the warehouse being thrown open. Instantly, the ring of several pairs of footsteps echoed hollowly through the building.

"Javen?" someone called loudly. "Answer me, boy. I'm here to help." Teagan recognized the worried voice of the elder Mr. Rotham. Still, she didn't move.

"Come on," Sir whispered soothingly. "You're a strong woman. Do this for me, Teagan."

And she did.

Sir flinched a little when the long needle punctured his skin, but Teagan's resolve held and she didn't remove the syringe until the last of the serum had been injected. Then she cast the empty needle aside. Pressing a palm to his chest, she found his heart still beat strongly. His breathing stayed steady. All this while, his eyes had followed her movements, and there was a light in them that said he was feeling stronger already.

The echoing voices and footsteps were coming closer to their little room.

Teagan ignored the intrusion on their privacy. "What happens now?" she asked, hovering anxiously by Sir's side.

"Now?" He smiled. "Now we keep no more secrets."

About the Author

Dara England lives in Oklahoma with her husband, two young daughters, and her beloved Yorkshire terrier. When she's not writing she's pouring over historical maps and biographies, watching period BBC shows, and chatting with other bibliophiles online.

She welcomes reader interaction and can be found at www.daraenglandauthor.com. While you're there, don't forget to sign up for her monthly newsletter!